North End Girl

Also by Karen A. Romanko

Television's Female Spies and Crimefighters

Women of Science Fiction and Fantasy Television

Historical Women on Television

North End Girl

Karen A. Romanko

Raven Electrick Ink

First edition, May 2025

ISBN: 978-0-9819643-6-2

Raven Electrick Ink
Los Angeles, California
contact@ravenelectrick.com

For my parents ...
and for Bob, always for Bob

Contents

Chapter 1

Do Me a Favor

"... we make our friends by conferring, not by receiving favors."

— Thucydides

Philip had asked her for *the* favor. Not just any favor, but the one her mother had told her never to do for anyone outside the family. Nicole's first mistake had been telling Philip she possessed the ability, but now he wanted her to use it. She had said she'd think it over, and give him an answer today, but she still hadn't decided. Nicole had two hours before they'd meet, and she was hoping for a sign, a blast of inspiration, anything that would tell her what to do.

Nicole punched in for work at Boston's Hotel Manger. She was an elevator operator at the hotel, and the job was unexciting for the most part. Up and down. Up and down. Up and down. But sometimes she got to meet performers and athletes who were working next door at Boston Garden. Roy Rogers had even brought his horse Trigger into the hotel! And once she had gotten her picture published in the *Boston Traveler*. A photographer had admired her wavy, black hair, and before she knew it, she was posing with a white rooster to publicize the Boston Poultry Show. But her fame, if you could call it that, was small and fleeting, and she was back to going up and down in her elevator the next day. Still, she had cut her picture out of the paper, and kept it in her pocketbook. She wondered whether that would be the only clipping she would ever have.

Right now the hotel staff was abuzz over the impending arrival of singer Teddy Messina and his young wife. Messina was considered a rising star of 1949. Nicole loved his songs, and had heard about his amazing blue eyes, although she had seen only black-and-white photos of him. Philip had blue eyes too, or more accurately blue-gray. She supposed those blue-gray eyes had been a big part of the reason she had revealed her secret to him.

Nicole knew that Philip would look for her in the break room later that morning, even though he had the day off. He was eager for an answer. He worked as a bellhop at the hotel, which gave him the run of the entire building. She was jealous to be stuck in her box all day, while he could see the wide world of the Charles River, Boston Harbor, and beyond from the top floors, but she also realized that he worked hard, seeing him frequently as he pushed luggage racks and hustled across the hotel lobby.

She arrived at her elevator, relieving the night girl, Carla. After exchanging a few pleasantries, Nicole got into the box and looked at the ceiling for inspiration. She found none, and people were entering the elevator, so she took them for a ride.

* * *

"How's my girl?" Philip reached under the table and grabbed Nicole's hand.

Am I his girl? She wondered. Philip was very handsome, and a lot of girls were interested in him. "I'm fine, Philip," she said with a little too much vinegar. She thought about moving her hand away, but she left it where it was.

"Have you decided, honey? I'm really hoping you can help me."

This was the moment of truth. "Oh, Philip, there is so much more at stake than I have explained to you. I really can't ..."

"Nicole, honey, you've got to help me with this. It's important for my future. Maybe *our* future."

She looked at those blue-gray eyes, and her resistance melted. "All right, I'll help you, but there could be consequences for me. You'll have to play this my way."

"Anything you say, honey." He squeezed her hand tight. "But we need to do it *soon.*"

Philip walked Nicole home to the North End of Boston. Nicole liked seeing him in his street clothes instead of that silly uniform with the pillbox hat. She wouldn't let him walk her to the door. He wasn't Italian, and she knew that would be an issue with her parents. Plus, she still wasn't sure where their relationship was going, so she'd wait to see what happened after she did him the favor.

"How close do you need to be?" Philip asked.

"How close ...? Oh, to Teddy, you mean? The closer, the better. If he gets in my elevator, that would be best, although it wouldn't give me long to read him."

"Well, the timing will be hard, because we won't know exactly when he's checking in. But you're bound to see him in your elevator at some point."

"Not necessarily. Stars have come and gone without my seeing them. They tend to be night people, and you know I work days. And there are elevators other than mine."

"Maybe you can sit in the lobby after work."

"For a while, but I'll be expected home before too long." She had so wanted to see Teddy Messina, and those blue eyes, but now a good part of her was hoping she'd miss him altogether, and this would be over.

"I know this is a big favor, although you haven't explained everything about why you don't want to use that ability of yours."

"To be honest, I don't understand everything myself." She thought about her mother's warning not to read the minds of boyfriends. Nicole wished all the rules were written down somewhere with explanations. She didn't know which were old wives' tales and which weren't. But she hadn't read Philip just in case. Finally she said, "How would you feel if I read *you*?"

"I don't think I'd like it very much."

"Well, one of the rules is not reading boyfriends, so I assume my mama knows what she's talking about."

"Sounds like it."

"Anyway, Teddy is due to check in tomorrow, so I will try to get something for you, if I see him." Philip had already sketched out his big plan. He was tired of being a bellhop, and was hoping to move up in guest relations. A recommendation from Teddy Messina or some other big shot would go a long way. Nicole was to read Teddy and pass on any information that might give Philip an edge.

"Great," Philip said. "I'm working a double shift tomorrow, so I'll be around all day."

They reached the corner of Baldwin Place. Philip looked around to see if anyone was peeking out the window over their flower boxes. All was clear, so he gave Nicole a quick goodbye peck on the cheek.

She smiled. "I'm not really sure how much help I can be, but I will give it a try. Don't get your hopes up."

"I know you will come through," he said.

After checking for prying eyes herself, she blew him a kiss as he walked away. She really did like Philip, so what was wrong with helping him out a little. Maybe she could get some inside information that would make him stand out to Teddy Messina. Everyone would win. Her mother's warnings still rang in her ears, but her mama tended to be a worrier. It would all work out.

* * *

Nicole didn't see Teddy Messina during her shift the next day. After she punched out, she sat in the lobby as close to the registration desk as she could get. Philip gave her a wink every time he passed.

She looked at her watch. She couldn't stay much longer, or she would have too much explaining to do at home. Suddenly she heard a commotion. Teddy Messina and his wife were coming through the door. Philip was behind them carrying luggage, and another bellboy, Joseph, was carrying some too. The couple stopped at reception. This was her chance.

Nicole focused on Teddy, trying to drown out all the distractions. He turned around and made eye contact once, which was a help. She waved, he smiled, and then she got down to business. *Well, let's see, he's tired. Not much we can do with that. He's not planning to do the town. Oh, he's interested in finding a poker game. That might be something Philip can use.*

She was feeling uncomfortable, and figured this morsel would be good enough. Teddy would go upstairs soon anyway, so she went over to Philip, who was waiting off to the side. She whispered, "He's looking for a poker game. Maybe you can help him find one. I've got to go home now."

Philip said, "Great! I know just what to tell him. Thanks, honey. I'll see you tomorrow."

Nicole turned around to leave and noticed a man, who

had been sitting opposite her. She didn't need to be a mind reader to know that he realized what she had done. She could tell by the expression of shock on his face. He was what her mother had called "a spotter," at least that was how Nicole had translated it into English. A spotter was not a mind reader per se, but someone whose only ability is recognizing mind readers when they use their powers. She quickly made her way into the "employees only" area of the hotel, so he couldn't follow her.

This wasn't good. Some people, especially criminals, were desperate to get hold of mind readers. Most of the population didn't believe the stories that occasionally circulated about mind readers, psychics, mentalists, whatever you wanted to call them, but the criminal element seemed more likely to accept the reports. Nicole wasn't sure why. *Maybe it's because they're always looking for an edge,* she thought. Who was this guy? Was she in danger? She went out a side door, and carefully worked her way around to the cab stand, looking out for the man constantly. She took a cab home, even though it was a short distance, using money she really couldn't spare. She should have listened to her mama.

Nicole arrived at work in a state of agitation the next day. She was tired after a restless night, but she was also vigilant, watching out for the man from yesterday or for anything out of the ordinary.

Philip met her in the break room at the usual time.

"What happened yesterday? You ran out the back so fast."

"Oh, Philip! My mother warned me, but I didn't listen. I guess there is no harm in telling you now." She explained about the spotter, and the danger to mind readers from people who might want to exploit their abilities.

"You should have told me, Nicole. My plan wasn't worth causing you trouble. Me and my big ideas."

"I didn't want to disappoint you, Philip. Plus, I wasn't sure how much of my mother's warning to believe. I haven't had my power all that long, so I don't have much experience. Women in my mother's family have had it for generations. That's the story, at least, but Mama doesn't have it herself. At this point, I'm not sure what's true and what isn't."

"I'm sorry," he said. "I wish I hadn't asked you. What did the guy look like? I can keep an eye out for him."

"He looks like a tough guy. A little bit like Humphrey Bogart, I guess."

"It may not be anything to worry about, honey. Maybe he's not even local. For all we know, he may have left the city."

"I hope so. Did you get anywhere with Teddy Messina?"

"Nah. I did ask him if he'd be interested in a poker game. His wife interrupted, mentioning his promise to take her to dinner at the hotel restaurant and spend the evening together. Teddy just shrugged, and that was that. By the way, you look a bit like her, especially close up."

"Mrs. Messina? I should be so pretty! But I guess we have similar hair."

"You are just as pretty," said Philip.

"I don't think so, but thank you ... honey." Nicole smiled. It was the first time she had called him that.

"You are a peach, honey, an absolute peach," Philip said.

The day passed without incident for Nicole. She never saw the guy who looked like "Bogie," and nothing unusual happened. While sometimes her job bored her, today it was a comfort. People were riding up and down in the elevator, keeping her company without their knowing it. In the afternoon, she answered a call to the top floor, and who should get on her elevator but Mrs. Messina.

"Hello, Mrs. Messina," she said. They were told to greet the hotel guests, using a personal touch whenever they could.

"Oh, please, call me 'Pat.' 'Mrs. Messina' makes me sound like an old woman."

"Okay, Pat. That's nice of you, but I will have to go back to 'Mrs.' if my boss is nearby."

"I understand. I hope they treat you well here."

Nice lady, Nicole thought. *She's just lovely.*

Nicole had to stop the elevator at a couple of floors on the way down to the lobby. She offered absent-minded greetings to the new passengers. She was focused on her one special guest.

The elevator reached the lobby at last. As Pat stepped

out, Nicole said, "I hope you enjoy your day." She had wanted to say something more captivating, but decided to play it safe.

"Thanks. I'm having a shopping afternoon at Jordan Marsh. Time to spend some of Teddy's money! I hope you have a nice day too. *Ciao!*"

"*Ciao!*" said Nicole.

Chapter 2

The Witch

"Behind every witch is a woman wronged."

— Alix E. Harrow

Pat Messina was looking forward to her day of shopping. She had heard that the Jordan Marsh department store was fabulous, and she wanted to check it out for herself. Pat would mostly browse, but she didn't plan to go back to the hotel empty-handed. *A new hat at the very least,* she thought, *and maybe some gloves.*

Mrs. Messina caught a cab outside the Hotel Manger, and told the driver to take her to Jordan's. As the taxi wound its way through some narrow streets, Pat looked out the window at a city she'd never seen before. They still hadn't hit a main thoroughfare, when the taxi started to lurch.

"Lady, something's wrong. I've got to pull over," the driver said.

"Oh, great," said Pat. *This trip is off to a bad start,* she thought.

The driver pulled the car into an alley.

Pat was already thinking she didn't like the look of this,

when a figure seemed to appear out of nowhere on the right. The door flew open, and Pat spotted a Halloween mask. She started to scream, but the figure's hand covered her mouth and a male voice said she'd better keep quiet. Pat looked at the other door, but the cab driver was blocking it, keeping his back to the window. The man in the mask, Popeye, she recognized, put a cloth bag over her head and yanked her from the taxi. She was pushed into another vehicle, where the engine was already running. The automobile began to move, making a sharp left turn, and seemed to enter into traffic, based on the speed of the car and the noise that reached her ears.

After a short ride, the car stopped. Someone pulled Pat out of the car, keeping hold of her arm. Another someone took the other arm, and they walked her for a few steps, probably on bricks. Her high heels didn't like the surface. The same voice from earlier said, "After we turn left, you need to walk down three stairs." She stumbled on the steps, but they held on to her. Eventually she found herself, still unable to see, sitting on a hard chair. She was most likely still in Boston, based on the distance driven, but otherwise had no idea where she was or who had grabbed her.

After who knows how long, Pat heard someone enter the room. The person spoke, a woman this time, with a bit of a Southern drawl. "I'm sure that hood is getting uncomfortable. I'm going to take it off on the condition that you play nice. I'm leaving you tied up for now. The more you cooperate, the more comfortable you will become. Do you understand?"

"Yes," said Pat. She felt the cloth bag sweeping off of her face. The room was poorly lit, with shades drawn and the only lamp not illuminated, so she couldn't see very well, but Pat realized the woman was wearing a Halloween mask. *A witch,* she thought. *How appropriate.*

"We need your help with something. We know about your special ability," said the lady wearing the mask.

"What special ability? My husband says I'm good at shopping. I'm sure that's not what you mean."

"Don't get funny. You seem like a nice kid. You can leave here a nice kid if you help us. I'll be bringing back someone with me. You're going to read him to help us out. Got it?"

"Okay." Pat wondered what the witch meant. *Read someone? Like a mind reader?* She figured it was best to play along. Maybe she could buy some time. "Yes, I can read someone for you."

"That's better. I'll be back later with a friend."

"I understand," said Pat. Teddy or the police wouldn't be looking for her yet. Teddy thought she was out happily shopping. She hoped it would take a good long while for the witch to come back with her friend. But Pat did need a bathroom. "Um, can I have a bathroom break?"

"You'll have to earn it." The witch turned and left.

What's happening here? Pat wondered. Minutes ago she was heading out on a shopping trip and now she was being held captive so she could read someone's mind. It was like some bizarre dream. The important thing, she realized, was to keep her wits about her. *Fight back the fear,* she told herself. Think positive thoughts. Well, the cloth bag was off of her head. That was something. One problem at a time.

Pat didn't know how much time had passed. She couldn't see her watch with her hands tied behind her. The room was totally dark now, so the sun must have set. She was achy from the bindings on her hands and feet, thirsty, and still in need of a bathroom.

Suddenly the door opened, and Pat saw a woman's form enter the room from an illuminated hallway. The woman disappeared in the dark, but Pat heard some footsteps and a click. The lamp in the corner radiated some light at last. The lady in the witch's mask was back.

Pat could see more clearly now. The lady was wearing not only the mask, but also a wig of long black hair. Clearly this woman did not want to be recognized. She also wore trousers with a matching jacket and gloves. This lady was a smart dresser.

"There's been a development," said the witch. "I don't suppose you can read someone who is unconscious."

"No. It requires a conscious mind." Pat was doing her best to play along with the scenario.

"We'll have to wait then."

"Can I go to the bathroom in the meantime?"

"I suppose so."

The witch stuck her head out the door, and called out, "Hey, uh ... Popeye, come in here!"

After a couple of minutes, a man in a Popeye mask entered the room. Popeye and the witch whispered for a few moments, and Pat couldn't hear them. Popeye grabbed the cloth hood from the lamp table and approached Pat. She felt the bag slipping over her head once again. Each of them grabbed one of her arms, taking her out of the room. Pat had to hop in her bindings. She heard a door open, and she had to hop a couple of more steps. One of them pulled off her hood, and then Popeye untied her hands and feet.

"Do your business," said the witch. "You can have a drink of water from the sink. We'll be outside. Use your momentary freedom wisely."

Pat did what she was told. She knocked on the door when she was finished, and they replaced the ties and the hood. They appeared to reverse the trip, and after opening a door, they removed the hood. Pat noticed a mattress on the floor. They helped her to her knees, and she positioned herself on the bed in as comfortable a position as she could. She knew this was the best she could do for the time being. A bathroom break, a drink of water, and a bed. Three more problems solved. Pat hoped someone would come to save her soon.

Chapter 3

Lila

"Adventure is just bad planning."

— Roald Amundsen

Lila removed her gloves, mask, and wig. *What a relief,* she thought. Although autumn had arrived, if one was to believe the calendar, the weather was still warm, and wearing those things made her perspire. Still, they were a necessity. As far as she knew, the police had heard whispers of her first name only, Lila, and they hadn't been able to put a face to that name. Lila wanted to keep it that way. Besides, the mind reader seemed like a nice kid, and she preferred to return her in good working order. Lila didn't like violence. She prided herself on finesse and planning.

Kidnapping the girl had gone without a hitch. The jeweler, Luftman, had been another matter. He was a little guy, and she hadn't expected him to put up much of a fight. When he did, Benny had knocked him out. Benny was good to have around, loyal to the end, but he didn't know his own strength. Now Luftman was lying unconscious in another room. Well, there was always an unexpected element in these things, so one had to expect the unexpected.

"Hey, Popeye, get in here!" Lila yelled down the hall.

The man in the Popeye mask entered the room.

"You can take that mask off, Benny. I know who you are."

"Okay, Lila." Benny slid the mask onto his head.

"How is our patient doing?"

"He's still out cold. Sorry, Lila. I shouldn't have had hit him so hard."

"These things happen, Benny. How is our other guest?"

"She seems to be resting uncomfortably."

"I hope we can wrap this up in the morning. Check on both of them every hour. If the jeweler regains consciousness, let me know immediately."

"Will do. Lila, have you ever seen *Lost Horizon?*

Oh, boy, Benny is about to go off on one of his tangents, Lila thought. "*Lost Horizon?* No, but I have read a book by that title. Probably the same story."

"There's a book?"

"Yes, Benny, a book."

"I'll have to see if the library has it. I don't know if the movie is the same, but in it the main characters crash land in Tibet and are taken to a special place called Shangri-La, where people never get sick or old. Doesn't that sound wonderful?"

"It does sound wonderful, Benny, but you could never leave that place, as I remember it. You wouldn't get old, but *it* would get old. You would be like a prisoner there. You couldn't go where you wanted, or you would die. That wouldn't be for me. I like my freedom."

"But you would be a Queen there, Lila. You could live forever," Benny said. "People would worship you."

Lila did not like the gleam in Benny's eye. She possessed the useful skill of keeping people off balance. Benny had the knack too, but he was making her feel uncomfortable now, and she didn't like it. Not one bit. "That's a nice thought, Benny, but you know it's just make-believe."

"I guess so."

"I'm getting a headache," Lila said, massaging her temples. I'm going to bed."

"Sorry, Lila. I hope you feel better soon. Goodnight."

"Remember not to fall asleep, Benny."

"Anything you say, Lila."

Chapter 4

The Demonstration

"... the truth is powerful and will prevail."

— Sojourner Truth

Nicole was feeling more relaxed when she arrived at work the next morning. Nothing unusual had happened the day before, so she hoped the guy who looked like Bogie had left town without telling anyone about her. She was about to clock in, when she saw a note on her timecard. It was from her boss, Mr. Altman, the hotel's assistant manager. Her feeling of relaxation evaporated. *What does he want? What did I do? Can this be related to the reading?* She punched in, and then looked down, smoothing out her uniform.

Nicole walked to Altman's office, which was not exactly plush, but at least resided in a nicer section of the "employees only" area. His door was open, but she knocked on it anyway.

"Come in, Nicole. Please take a seat. I won't keep you long. We have had an unfortunate incident here at the hotel. Patricia Messina, the wife of singer Teddy Messina, has gone missing. Her husband hasn't seen her since yesterday afternoon when she left for shopping."

"Oh, no! I'm so sorry," said Nicole. "She told me in the elevator that she was planning to go shopping."

"I'm sure the police will want to hear that information. They are investigating this as a missing person's case. Lieutenant Fitzgerald is in charge, and he is questioning staff members in the lounge. We have temporarily roped off the area. You should go see him at once. Carla will cover for you in the elevator until you are finished. I have assured the lieutenant every cooperation from our staff."

Nicole's thoughts were racing, but she managed to say, "Okay, I'll go see him now." She searched her mind for how Pat's disappearance might be related to her reading. She didn't see any connection, but it definitely qualified as an unusual occurrence just one day after the spotter had noticed her. Nicole hoped it was just a coincidence, and she prayed that Pat was all right. She headed to the lounge.

A man stood in front of the ropes that temporarily cordoned off the area. Nicole stopped, assuming she needed to check in.

"Yes, Miss?"

"I was told by my supervisor, Mr. Altman, to come here. I'm supposed to talk to Lieutenant Fitzgerald."

"What's your name, please?"

"Nicole, well, that should be Nicolina ... Nicolina Rossi, but I prefer Nicole."

The man looked down at his notebook. "Okay, Miss

Rossi. Please wait with the others. The lieutenant will call you when he's ready for you."

Nicole seated herself on one of the plush chairs that lined the wall opposite the staircase. The Manger's lounge was a beautiful spot, with its painted murals and rose-tinted marble. It was nice to have a chance to sit here, except, of course, for the circumstances. She recognized the other hotel workers present, although she didn't know all of them personally. She waved to George from the front desk, who waved back. Everyone was so quiet that Nicole felt like she was in church. *They're probably all nervous*, she thought. Police didn't come to investigate a kidnapping every day, even at the Hotel Manger.

A man Nicole hadn't seen before was sitting at one of the desks at the far wall. That was probably Lieutenant Fitzgerald. What was going on? What had happened to poor Pat? Nicole tried to sort things out in her mind, but nothing made sense. This couldn't have anything to do with the favor she had done for Philip. *It just couldn't.*

The man at the desk finally called her name. Nicole arose from her chair and approached him. She had never talked to a detective before, and she was trying to keep her nerves in check.

"Hello, Miss Rossi. I am Lieutenant Fitzgerald."

"Hello, Lieutenant."

He shook her hand. "Please take a seat. I have just a few questions for you. I hope not to keep you here too long. As I'm sure you have heard, Teddy Messina's wife, Patricia, has been reported missing. Did you have any contact with her yesterday?"

Nicole was afraid she was going to burst into tears, but she tried to control herself. "Yes, I did take her down in my elevator yesterday."

"Do you remember what time that was?"

"It was in the afternoon, sometime after 2 PM, I think."

"Did she talk to you at all?"

"Yes, she told me to call her 'Pat,' and she mentioned she was planning to go shopping at Jordan Marsh."

"Good, that's helpful." Fitzgerald jotted something down. "Did she seem at all upset about anything?"

"No, she was very friendly and seemed like she was looking forward to her shopping trip."

"Anything else that comes to mind about the conversation?"

"That's all I can think of."

"Did you see her at any time after that?"

"No, that was the only time."

"Well, that should do it then. Thanks for helping us. If you think of anything else, you can find me here for the next few hours." Fitzgerald checked Nicole's name off his list, and glanced at the photo of Patricia Messina in front of him. "Hey, you sort of look like her."

"Do I? My ... uh ... friend ... says that too."

"I agree with your friend."

"Thank you, Lieutenant." Nicole rose from her chair to

leave. She heaved a sigh of relief as she walked away, hoping that was the end of her part in the case.

Nicole met Philip in the break room as usual. He was already seated at a table in the corner, where they could speak more privately. Pushing a cup of tea towards her side of the table, he said, "How are you doing, honey? You look upset."

"Well, it's been an upsetting morning," she said. "First the news about Pat Messina. I just saw her on the elevator yesterday. She was so nice! Then having to talk to the police lieutenant. He was polite, but this is all so nerve-racking. Have you spoken with him yet?"

"I'm supposed to see him right after this."

After taking a sip of her tea, Nicole said, "Thanks for this, by the way. I keep thinking Pat's kidnapping might have something to do with the favor I did for you, and especially the spotter I told you about. But I can't see what the connection is."

"I think you should put that out of your mind, Nicole. Famous people or their family members do go missing sometimes."

"Yes, but the timing was just so close."

"There is such a thing as a coincidence."

"That's true. You know, Lieutenant Fitzgerald also mentioned that I look like Pat."

"See, I told you."

"Do you think that could be it? What if someone thought she was me, and grabbed her?"

"That doesn't seem likely."

"Wait a minute. I am remembering something my mother told me. She said that a spotter can't see the face of a mind reader very well during a reading. It's like a haze or an aura or something. Maybe Bogie pointed out the wrong person to someone!"

"I don't know, honey."

"And she was wearing a dark blue suit. It looked something like my uniform."

"Nicole ..."

"But if they did take her instead of me, I have to figure out a way to help. I guess I could talk to the lieutenant again. I could see him during my lunch break."

"I don't know about that," Philip said. "How would you explain?" He gave Nicole's hand a squeeze under the table. "Do what you think is best for you, honey. You really don't need to involve yourself in this."

"But what if I am involved already? I don't think I have a choice."

"It sounds like you've already decided. I'm not sure the police are going to believe you. Just think about it a little more."

"Okay. I'll think about it some more," she said, but she was already wondering how she was going to tell Fitzgerald. Would he even listen?

* * *

Nicole returned to the hotel lounge during her lunch break. She talked to the man in front of the ropes again, and he allowed her to pass. Taking a seat on the sofa in the middle of the lounge, Nicole thought about what she was going to tell Lieutenant Fitzgerald. There really was no way to explain things without revealing the existence of her power. Her mother had told her not to tell anyone, and now she was going to tell a second person, not to mention the spotter who had found out on his own, and any people he might have told. Maybe she would end up with another newspaper clipping after all, but not the kind she or her family would want. What a mess! But Pat's life might be at stake, so she needed to do this for her.

After calling her name, Fitzgerald said, "Hello, Miss Rossi. Did you remember something else?"

"Well, in a way." Nicole launched into her story, and Fitzgerald seemed to raise his eyebrows higher with each new revelation.

At last he said, "That is some tale. I'm not going to dismiss it out of hand, first, because you do resemble Mrs. Messina, second, because we have heard rumors about such abilities, and, third, because I pride myself on keeping an open mind. I'm simply going to give you a chance to demonstrate your mind reading ability. If you are successful, we will speak further. If you're not, I will ask you not to waste my time ever again. Do you wish to proceed?"

Nicole was afraid her nerves would get in the way of the test, but she said, "Yes, I will try, but given what happened last time, I don't want to do this out in the open, where people can see me."

Fitzgerald looked around. There was a small alcove under the stairway that led down into the lounge. He said, "What about over there?"

Nicole turned around to inspect it. The alcove wouldn't provide much cover, but if she tucked herself in the back and he stood in front of her, it would probably be all right. "I guess that will work," she said.

They took the few steps to the alcove, and Nicole tried to hide herself as much as possible.

Fitzgerald said, "Okay, let's give this a try. What's the name of my son's goldfish?"

Nicole would have laughed, but none of this was funny. She looked Fitzgerald straight in the eyes and tried to read his thoughts. His disbelief was practically screaming at her, so it was hard to penetrate that, but she finally said, "The fish's name is Alfalfa."

"What? Um ... that is correct. How did you ... Well, I guess you could have gotten that from someone I know. I'll have to think of something I've never told anyone." He paused for a minute. "Okay, I've got something."

Nicole focused on Fitzgerald's eyes again. His disbelief was no longer yelling, and it had been joined by some wonder as well. She tried to get below those and was surprised at what she found. "You wish you hadn't stolen money from your mother's jewelry box. She never told your father so he wouldn't punish you."

Fitzgerald was quiet at first. At last he said, "This is unbelievable. I've never told anyone that. My mother was the only one who knew."

Nicole smiled. "It is unbelievable, but I'm glad you gave me the chance to show you I wasn't lying."

"With this new, um, information, I have to admit that there might be something to your mistaken identity theory, but we have to keep this between us for the moment."

"That's just fine with me. I was going to ask if you could do that anyway."

"I'm not sure how this development would play downtown, but I will keep it in mind as I search for motives. In the meantime, I still have to pursue other possibilities."

"I understand."

"Given your unique ability, you may be able to help me as the case progresses. Are you willing to do that?"

"Yes, as long as I can help Pat, but I would need to stay in the background."

"That's the way we'll play it. I will contact you here, if I need to talk to you. Thank you for coming forward. It was a brave thing to do under your special circumstances."

"Thank you, Lieutenant."

Nicole felt much better as she returned to work. She had done the right thing, and she hoped the information would help the police find Pat. Poor Pat. What was she going through?

Chapter 5

Jack

"Aging is not 'lost youth' but a new stage of
opportunity and strength."

— Betty Friedan

Jack Fitzgerald decided to take a break after the strange turn of events with Miss Rossi. He went to find a men's room, and checked to see if it was empty. After splashing some water on his face, he said out loud, "What the hell was that?" Fitzgerald liked talking to himself. It made him feel less alone.

He looked in the mirror. Fitzgerald was 45 years old, but looked 55. Well, the life of a cop would do that to you. And this new problem would probably add another year to the tally. What was he going to do about Nicole Rossi? Granted, Rossi could prove to his superiors that she had the ability to read minds, but who knows what would happen to her once the higher-ups found out. He needed to keep his mouth shut. On the other hand, if this case turned out to be linked to her, how was he going to explain that. This whole thing was giving him a headache, the kind that felt like his head would split into two halves. It always happened when he was conflicted about something.

Then he got an idea. Yes, he would keep it to himself, at least for now, but this development also presented an opportunity. He knew what he would do.

Fitzgerald left the men's room and headed for the hotel lobby. As he'd hoped, Rossi was standing in her elevator, waiting for passengers. He hopped on and said, "Let's go for a ride."

Nicole said, "What floor, please?"

"Take us to the top, and no stops."

Nicole looked startled, but did what she was told.

"Miss Rossi, I'm going to need your help with the case for a little longer. What time do you get off work?"

"Um, 4 PM."

"Can you spare a little time for me after that?"

"I have plans with my friend. How much time would you need?"

"No more than 30 minutes, I would think."

"Okay, that's about all I would be able to spare."

"Great. Look for me in the lounge after you clock out from work."

When they reached the top floor, he said, "Take us back down."

Nicole appeared in the hotel lounge a few minutes after 4 PM, as promised. The man at the ropes let her pass without question, and Fitzgerald waved her over.

"Miss Rossi, please have a seat. Let me explain my plan. In a few minutes I'm going upstairs to Teddy Messina's suite for a second interview. I haven't forgotten what you told me earlier, and I'm taking it seriously, but, as I mentioned, I do need to pursue other lines of inquiry. In this type of case, we need to look closely at the spouse. If we can eliminate that person as a suspect, we can move ahead to follow other leads. Are you with me so far?"

"I think so."

"Good. I would like you to accompany me ..."

Nicole gasped.

"... I would like you to accompany me to Mr. Messina's suite. You will appear to be there as my stenographer, on loan from the hotel. Can you take shorthand?"

"I had a course in school, but it wasn't my best subject."

"As long as you can fake it, you'll be fine. In reality, I would like you to read Messina's mind as I interview him. I know this is a lot to ask, but you've already read him once, so there shouldn't be any objection on that score. And if we can eliminate him as a suspect, you will also be helping his wife."

"I'm not sure what to say. I want to help, but I'm going to be so nervous. I'm not much of an actress."

"You seem to be a strong young woman. I think you'll do fine. Just say hello to him, and then pretend to be consumed by your work. I think he'll buy it."

"I don't know about that, but I will try."

"Excellent."

Fitzgerald turned away from Nicole and looked over at the man guarding the ropes. "Reese, can I see you for a second?"

"Yeah, boss."

"I'm just about done here. I'm going to talk one more time to Messina in his suite before I leave. You can head out now."

"Great. See you tomorrow, boss," Reese said, and then "goodbye, Miss Rossi."

"Goodbye," she said.

"As promised," Fitzgerald said, "I'm keeping this just between the two of us."

Nicole sighed, but nodded.

"Let's head upstairs," he said.

"Please come in," said Teddy Messina.

"Thank you," Lieutenant Fitzgerald said. "This is Miss Rossi. I've borrowed her from the hotel to serve as stenographer, so we don't have to send for a girl from the station."

"How do you do, Miss Rossi."

"Oh ... nice to meet you ... Mr. Messina."

Fitzgerald watched as Nicole blushed. He hoped she wasn't going to blow his whole scheme.

"Lieutenant, have you made any progress in finding my

wife?"

"Let's sit down," said Fitzgerald, "and we can talk."

Nicole sat on a soft chair, and opened her steno pad. She looked around the lavish suite, and seemed curious, but her eyes snapped back to the pad.

Good, thought Fitzgerald. *She's playing along.*

"Mr. Messina, we have talked to everyone on the hotel staff who might have seen your wife yesterday. Someone has corroborated your story of her leaving for a shopping trip after 2 PM." Fitzgerald found it hard to resist looking at Nicole, but he tried not to signal that she was the witness. "We have also talked to taxi drivers outside, none of whom claim to have seen her. A couple of our men have visited the Jordan Marsh department store, but no one there recognized her photo. Of course, they deal with many shoppers per day, and they have multiple entrances, so it is quite possible she could still have visited the store. I'd like to ask you if your wife might have been upset about anything when she left. Please understand that I need to ask such a question in the course of an investigation like this."

"I'm not offended, Lieutenant. Pat was excited about her shopping trip, happy to be in Boston, and didn't seem upset about anything."

"Another question I have to ask," said Fitzgerald. "Is there anyone who might have a grudge against you or your wife? Or someone who might do this as a prank?"

"There's no one I can think of. Pat is a doll, and

everyone loves her. Well, a few of my female fans might be jealous," Messina said, glancing quickly in Nicole's direction, "but I doubt any of them would stoop to that level. As for me, I have a bit of a temper, and I'm a perfectionist, but I don't mistreat the people who work with me."

"Have you received any threats?"

"Sometimes guys will get aggressive when I'm out on the town, calling me 'a pretty boy' and trying to show how tough they are, but I have never received any threats by mail or phone."

Fitzgerald looked at Nicole, who was scratching away at her pad. She was doing a good job of faking it. He hoped she hadn't forgotten about the main reason why she was there.

As if reading Fitzgerald's mind, Nicole glanced at him.

He flinched, surprising himself. *Is she reading MY mind too*, he wondered, *a two-for-one special?* Maybe he should have considered this plan more carefully. He was a novice in this world of psychic abilities, and who knew what he was getting himself into. *No*, he thought, *she seems like a good kid. Trust your instincts*. He turned back to the singer.

"Mr. Messina, I'm sure you would have told us, but have you received a ransom demand?"

"No ransom demand," said Teddy. "What happens next?"

"We will question more cab drivers tonight and continue canvassing the area. Someone will have seen something."

"I hope so," said Messina. "She means the world to me, my Patty." He looked away.

"I'm sorry," said Fitzgerald. He watched as Nicole wiped her eyes. "I think that's all we have for now. Please alert us immediately if you receive a ransom demand or think of any other information that might be useful. You already have my card."

"Thank you, Lieutenant. Good evening to you both."

After shaking hands again and saying goodbye, Fitzgerald and Nicole left the suite. Nicole started to talk, but Fitzgerald pressed a finger to his lips. They called for the elevator, and Nicole greeted a twilight shift operator, Renata. It was a quiet ride down, with stops on several floors. As they reached the bottom, Fitzgerald said to Nicole, "Let's talk in the lounge." Nicole looked at her watch, and then nodded.

Although the sentry had gone home, the lounge was still roped off. Fitzgerald opened the rope for Nicole, and then followed her. They seated themselves on opposite sides of the corner desk again.

"You did very well, Miss Rossi."

"Thank you, Lieutenant. I was so nervous."

"Was he telling the truth?"

"I hope you were able to get some information for me."

"It was difficult with so many emotions in my head and so many emotions in *his* head, but I was able to make a connection."

"Yes, as best I could tell. I'm new to all of this, but he

seems to love his wife and is concerned about her welfare. I don't think he knows where she is."

"That's good to hear. For all I know, the guy's an actor as well as a singer, and actors can fake the grieving husband thing."

"I think he is sincere."

"I think so too, but it is nice to have your special type of corroboration. By the way, I hope you weren't tempted to read me while you were at it."

"Lieutenant! Reading people has gotten me into enough trouble already."

"I see your point. It's just a strange new world for me."

"Me too. I'd like to leave now, if we're finished."

"Yes, we're done. Thank you for your help. Have a nice evening with your friend."

Nicole said goodbye and departed. Fitzgerald wondered whether he'd done the right thing in taking advantage of her ability, but consoled himself with the thought that using the fastest route was always best in a missing persons case.

Chapter 6

Stalling for Time

"Improvisation is too good to leave to chance."

— Paul Simon

Pat Messina found herself awake. She was sure she hadn't slept much, dozing off for what seemed like a few minutes here and there. She had never been so uncomfortable in her life, with her hands and feet bound throughout the night.

The room had taken on some light, so she assumed the new day had broken. Her dear Teddy would know she was missing by now. What must be going through his mind? She hoped someone would come for her soon.

The door to the room opened, but it wasn't the someone she was hoping for. The masked witch and Popeye were back, and they had brought another captive. The person, apparently a man based on the physique, was tied like Pat, and wearing a hood.

The witch said, "Good morning. I hope you slept well. Our friend here is now conscious, so we should be able to complete our business. Cooperate, and we will be able to return you safe and sound to your husband. We need you to do your little trick on this gentleman. He is expecting a shipment of diamonds, and you will tell us all the details so we can, uh, expedite them to a different location. If your information pans out, we will arrange to have you returned to the Manger."

Pat began to panic. She started to run through her options at breakneck speed. She could fake a reading and give the witch an answer to buy some time. But what would they do to her when they found out she was lying? What would they do to her anyway? Or she could try to stall. "I will do what I can," said Pat.

The witch pulled the hood off of Pat's fellow captive. "Okay, show us what you got."

Pat saw the bruised face of a middle-aged man who looked terrified. Trying to keep her wits about her, she said, "This will work better if I can sit up and face him."

"Popeye, go and help the young lady to a chair."

Popeye did what he was told, and Pat was soon seated upright.

"I'm not sure I will succeed under these conditions, but here goes," Pat said. She looked into the man's eyes and then closed hers. Instead of reading him, she was recalling techniques she had learned in the acting classes Teddy had paid for. Who knew she would be using them this way? "I'm not getting anything but fear from him. I'm sorry."

"Well, try harder," said the witch.

Pat looked into the man's eyes again, and pretended to

concentrate. "That's all I'm getting. Fear. You know, this isn't an exact science, and I am in pain, tired, starving, and I need a bathroom. I might do better if my body wasn't distracting me so much."

The woman in the witch's mask said, "Another delay. Beautiful. All right, I see your point. Popeye, after we return him to his room and take her to the bathroom, go find this young lady some food. Once you've eaten, little mind reader, I'm expecting some big things from you."

Popeye put the bag over the man's head and they escorted him from the room in silence.

Pat had bought herself a little more time. Would it do her any good? At least she had been promised a bathroom and some food. Maybe things would look better after that.

Chapter 7

Plan B (Or Is It C?)

"Opportunity makes a thief."

— Francis Bacon

"Benny, make me some toast too."

"Okay, Lila," he said. Benny started whistling while he made toast and tea in the cramped kitchen of their current headquarters, a basement apartment in a Beacon Hill row house.

What a peculiar man, thought Lila. *He beats up a guy and then he makes toast and tea.* He was useful, she had to say that.

Benny placed a teacup in front of Lila. "Toast is coming right up," he said.

"Thanks, Benny. What would I do without you?"

Benny blushed.

Yes, peculiar, Lila thought.

Benny delivered her toast, and made a tray for their guest. He started to leave the kitchen, and Lila said, "Benny, your mask!"

"Oh ... right, Lila."

"And untie her hands *only*, not her feet."

"Got it!"

Lila shook her head, then started on her toast and tea. Grabbing the morning newspaper, she scanned the headlines. Some print on the lower page caught her eye.

Singer's Wife Reported Missing

"What the ..." Lila exclaimed. She read the story. Patricia Messina, wife of singer Teddy Messina, had never returned to the Hotel Manger after a shopping trip on Wednesday. Police were investigating. The accompanying photo showed that the woman currently in Lila's possession was Mrs. Messina. Lila looked back at the newspaper story. She had heard of the singer, who seemed to be popular with the younger set, especially teenage girls.

Maybe there was another angle to play here, Lila thought. A ransom demand might be in order. Get more seed money and then do the diamond job. That Messina fellow, a famous singer, should be good for a bundle. Lila would have to decide how much. Things were looking up!

Benny came back with the tray from Mrs. Messina's room.

"I set her up at the table," he said. "I kept her feet tied, like you asked."

"Good man! Guess what, Benny? We've been entertaining a celebrity! Our guest is Patricia Messina, wife of singer Teddy Messina."

"Ooh, I like him!"

"I'm happy for you, Benny."

"What are we going to do, Lila?"

"We are moving to plan B. Or is it C? We're going to send a ransom note to Mrs. Messina's husband. Let's go tell her the good news."

Lila entered the room in her witch's mask and wig. "Hello, Mrs. Messina. I hope you enjoyed your breakfast."

"Mrs Messina? How did you find out?"

"You've made the paper, darling. Are you really a mind reader or have you just been playing along? Let's find out! What's my name?"

She watched as Messina stared into her eyes, probably a little difficult with the witch's mask in the way, but she had heard that these mind readers had astounding abilities.

"I'm sorry. I'm not getting anything. Maybe ..."

"No more excuses. Try again! What's the name of my friend in the Popeye mask?"

Her guest turned her attention to Benny. Being Benny, he did something peculiar, swaying and muttering.

"I'm still not ..."

"You understand, there's no advantage to you in holding back."

"I understand," said Pat. She started to sob.

"Ah, all becomes clear," said Lila. "Well, it was fun, while it lasted. I must admit you did a fine job of playing along. I'm guessing you have had some training in acting. We will have to update our plans once again. Now your husband will have to pay to get you back. He loves you, no? Will do anything to have you back in his arms? I will try to expedite this process so you can return to him as soon as possible."

Lila tried to read the look on her captive's face. It was hard to tell whether Messina was relieved by the news or not. Yes, a mentalist would definitely come in handy, but she'd have to wait for one a little longer.

Back in the kitchen, Lila said to Benny, "Wait until I see that spotter, Garrison! He must have identified the wrong woman. What a colossal screwup! Well, at least the one we've got has some ransom value. We will have to postpone the diamond job until we can find the real mind reader."

Now Lila had two captives and neither one of them could read minds. She couldn't take in the psychic at the moment anyway. There was no room at the inn, so to speak. But she needed to get something out of all her work so far. A ransom demand it would be.

Chapter 8

Thursday Night Date

"Lead the audience by the nose to the thought."

— Laurence Olivier

Nicole looked for Philip at the Hotel Manger's coffee shop. Her parents knew she had a regular Thursday evening date with work friends to have a bite to eat at the coffee shop and then see a movie. What they didn't know was that sometimes her friend was a girlfriend, and sometimes it was Philip. Nicole realized she was deceiving them, but it wasn't technically a lie, since Philip was a work friend.

She was glad Philip wasn't on duty tonight. She wished they could eat in the Manger's Main Dining Room, with its mirror-panelled walls and beamed ceiling, but it was too much of an extravagance on their wages. Nicole often insisted on going Dutch for these Thursday night outings, although Philip always offered to pay. It helped to convince her that she wasn't lying to her parents.

Nicole spotted Philip at a corner table and waved. She rushed over and took the seat opposite him.

"Hi!"

"Hello! How did it go with Fitzgerald?" he asked.

Nicole leaned in and lowered her voice. "He said I did well. I was very anxious, and it was hard to concentrate on mind reading while pretending to be a stenographer, but I managed to carry it off. I felt so bad for Teddy Messina. He seems to love his wife and knows nothing about where she is ..."

Their waitress interrupted. It was June, not one of Nicole's favorites. "What'll you have, kids?"

"I'll have apple pie and black coffee," said Philip.

"I'll have apple pie too, but I'd like tea with milk, please," Nicole said.

June made a few notes on her pad, and winked at Philip, before heading to the kitchen.

Nicole rolled her eyes. "Anyway, I hope I'm done with the case, although I wouldn't mind seeing Teddy again under better circumstances."

Now it was Philip's turn to roll his eyes.

Nicole gave his arm a love tap. "You know what I mean! I finally get a chance to talk to a popular singer, and it's under completely horrible circumstances."

"I know." Philip said. "Well, this is all we've been talking about lately. Let's focus on us. Do you still want to go to the Paramount tonight?"

"Of course! I'm looking forward to spending some time with you outside of this place. They're showing *My Friend Irma*. Can't wait! I love the radio show. I hope the movie will be as good. And I think John Lund is dreamy!"

Philip offered up another eye roll and then conspicuously stared at Nicole's hand. She received his message loud and clear, placing her hand under the table, where his fingers found hers.

Thank goodness for Thursday night dates, she thought.

Nicole and Philip boarded an MTA train at North Station and took it three stops to Winter Street. The train was crowded at that hour, so they had to stand. Nicole held on to one of the hanging straps for balance, but Philip used the situation as an opportunity to hold on to her. They both laughed.

Emerging from the Winter Street subway station, the couple walked down to Washington Street, turning right. Nicole winced when she saw Jordan Marsh's department store, remembering Pat Messina's enthusiasm about her planned shopping trip there.

"What's wrong, honey?" asked Philip.

"Oh, seeing Jordan Marsh reminded me of Pat Messina. Why did she have to go missing?"

"I'm sorry, Nicole. I hope they find her soon. But, remember, we were going to focus on us and having a nice evening."

"You're right. I'll do my best to put it out of my mind."

"That's better."

Nicole and Philip continued to the Paramount Theater, where they bought their tickets, picked up some popcorn for Philip, and settled themselves in a back row on the main floor. Nicole loved looking at the design of the theater, noticing sunburst patterns everywhere she turned, especially the big ones, above the movie screen and on the ceiling. She had heard that the style used throughout the theater was called Art Deco. It was stunning, and made Nicole feel like she was visiting a palace.

While Philip enjoyed his snack, Nicole turned her attention to the other moviegoers, who marched at a steady pace down the aisle. She spotted a blonde woman, who was wearing too much makeup, in Nicole's opinion, at least. The blonde was holding the arm of a man, who .... She gasped. "Philip, that's him!"

"Him, who?"

"The man!" She thought to lower her voice. "The spotter," she whispered. "The one who looks like Humphrey Bogart."

"Where?"

"He's down in front now. With that blonde. They are about to take their seats. What should we do?"

"Maybe we shouldn't do anything."

"But he may have some information that will lead to finding Pat Messina."

"I guess. What do you want to do?"

"After they are settled, let's move closer. Maybe I can

read him and get something useful for Lieutenant Fitzgerald."

"Will he know he's being read?"

"I don't know! Maybe not, if he can't see me. I'm not sure how this works, but I know I should try."

"All right, let's move down, but we'll stay a few rows behind them."

"Thank you, Philip. I know this isn't the evening we planned."

"And I haven't forgotten that I got you into this in the first place."

She squeezed his hand.

They chose seats a few rows back from the spotter, and almost directly behind him, so he would be less likely to see them if he turned around. They had to crawl over a few people in the row, as the theater was beginning to fill.

"I think I should do it now, before the movie begins, " said Nicole. "The fewer distractions, the better." She tried to focus, although seeing his face would have helped. It took some time, maybe 45 seconds, for her to receive his signal, so to speak. All of a sudden, Bogie turned around, his eyes searching the auditorium. Philip grabbed Nicole and kissed her. Nicole caught on that he was trying to hide her face, but she allowed herself to get lost in the moment. After they broke, she said, "I guess he could feel me reading him. We should leave as soon as the movie starts."

"I think we'd better. That was creepy. So much for our date."

"We still have time tonight," she whispered. "Let's talk about it when we get outside."

Nicole and Philip waited until the film had started, and people were so caught up in their laughter that they wouldn't notice a young couple leaving early. The two of them tried to move as quietly as possible, so they wouldn't cue Bogie to their departure. Once outside, they walked swiftly away from the theater, turning around frequently to see if they were being followed. At last Nicole said, "I think we're in the clear. Let's walk up to Boston Common. My parents won't be expecting me yet, so there's no need for the date to end right now. Is that okay with you?"

"That's fine with me. As long as we can spend some time together. Well, that was certainly a weird situation. Did you get anything from the spotter?"

"Maybe. I got two names, Lila and Benny. They seemed to be connected to an image of diamonds. Then there was something odd. A witch's Halloween mask. I'm not sure how much that will help Fitzgerald, but I will tell him."

"A Halloween mask? Yeah, that's probably not related, but Fitzgerald may recognize those names. Okay, let's make that the end of this discussion for tonight. Deal?"

"Deal!"

Nicole took Philip's arm as they walked up Temple Place. They reached Tremont Street and crossed to Boston Common, where they strolled along its paths without any particular direction in mind. After a few twists and turns, they found themselves at the Frog Pond, where kids swam during the summer. The evening was cool, but the wind was calm, so they searched for a bench where they could rest for a while. Nicole thought it would be a good chance for them to talk without worrying about being overheard for a change, but the prospect made her skittish at the same time. She and Philip really hadn't spent much time alone. Nicole wanted to stay clear of the kidnapping subject, which continued to muscle its way into her thoughts, so she decided a discussion about movies might be a safe way to get the conversation rolling.

"Who are your favorite actors?" she asked.

"Hmm ... I don't know many names," Philip said. "Let me think. Lauren Bacall. She's really something."

"I like her too. Her looks are so striking. Do you remember her line from *To Have and Have Not?* "You know how to whistle, don't you, Steve? You just put your lips together and ... blow.""

"That's right! Hey, you did that pretty well. Who else do you like?"

"I loved Fred MacMurray in *Double Indemnity*. He's so handsome, but seeing that movie was a strange experience. I was rooting for him, even though I knew he had helped to commit the murder. He just made the character so likable. Does that make me a bad person?"

"Of course not. You could never be a bad person."

"You're sweet," Nicole said, squeezing Philip's hand. Her plan was working, so she pushed ahead. "I really like mysteries and crime films. I also enjoyed *Out of the Past* with Robert Mitchum. And *Laura* starring Gene Tierney. She's another great beauty. These films aren't very happy, but they're up my alley for some reason. Maybe my feelings about them will change after this real-life brush with crime we're going through. Oh ... I didn't mean to talk about it again.

"That's okay! It's bound to come up. Just keep going. Your memory is amazing."

Nicole started to rattle off actors and movies until she forgot the reason they had fled to the Common. She stopped for a second, wondering if she was talking too much, and whether she should ask Philip if he wanted to change the subject. He kissed her then, and Nicole thought maybe he had read *her* mind.

Chapter 9

A Ransom Demand

"Have more than thou showest,

Speak less than thou knowest ..."

— William Shakespeare

Lieutenant Jack Fitzgerald arrived at the Hotel Manger a little after 9 AM. It seemed like he was spending all his time there. Fitzgerald was about to pay a call on Teddy Messina in a deluxe suite. The singer had finally received a ransom demand for his wife, Patricia, after her disappearance two days earlier.

Fitzgerald approached the elevators and saw Miss Rossi. She waved and stepped out of the box.

"Good morning, Miss Rossi. I can't seem to stay away from this place."

"Hello, Lieutenant. I need to speak with you. I may have ... um ... come across ... some information that might help you."

"I'd love to hear it, but not just now. I'm already late for an appointment with Mr. Messina. Can I speak with you later? When is your break?"

"It's at 10 AM."

"Okay, can you meet me in the lounge at 10?"

"Well, I'm supposed to meet my friend, but I will cancel it. I'll be there."

"Very good. Please take me to the top. You know the way."

Fitzgerald emerged on the 17th floor, and headed toward Messina's suite. A ransom demand wasn't necessarily good news, but at least it was some forward movement. He knocked on the door, and Messina opened it. The singer's face was ashen, and he held a large piece of paper in his hand.

"Lieutenant, thank you for coming. Here is the note I received."

Taking the paper from Messina, Fitzgerald stepped into the suite. The letters on the ransom note had been cut out from newspaper headlines. The message read:

WE HAVE YOUR WIFE.
IT WILL COST YOU $100,000
TO GET HER BACK.
WAIT FOR INSTRUCTIONS.

"How did you receive this?" asked Fitzgerald.

"I found it near the door this morning. I assumed it had been slipped underneath."

"Right. It's possible, of course, that someone read the story about your wife in the newspaper and is trying to take advantage of the situation. There's not a lot to go on here, unfortunately, but I would like to take this back to the department for analysis. Can you put together this amount, if necessary?"

"It won't be easy, but I am already working on it. My father-in-law is helping too."

"Good. It's unlikely they will contact you in the same way again, because they will assume we are watching your suite now. I'm guessing the next contact will be by phone. I have an interview to conduct downstairs, but I'll check back with you as soon as I can. In the meantime, I'm going to station Detective Reese here. He's a good man. We will need to ask these people for proof that they actually have Mrs. Messina, and, I'm sorry to say this, that she is alive."

"I will pay everything I have to get her back."

"I understand. But we need to make sure they have her and that this isn't just a con. You want to be certain you are giving the money to the actual kidnappers."

Teddy burst into tears.

Fitzgerald put his hand on the singer's shoulder. "I'm sorry, Mr. Messina. I understand how difficult this must be for you. I will be sending Reese right up. He is talking to another cab driver downstairs. I'll return as soon as I can. We're going to do everything in our power to see that your wife is safely returned to you."

"Thank you, Lieutenant."

Fitzgerald left Messina's suite and called for the elevator. It arrived promptly, and Miss Rossi greeted him again.

"Hello, Nicole. We'll have to stop meeting like this." He chuckled. Miss Rossi's elevator was one of two assigned to cover floors 10 through 17 of the hotel, making their meetings more likely. "By the way, do you mind if I call you by your first name? Miss Rossi is starting to seem a bit formal."

"I don't mind, Lieutenant."

"Jack. Why don't you call me Jack?"

"All right, Jack."

"That's better. I'm still planning to see you at 10. I've got to go talk to Reese for a minute. He'll be coming up here."

Nicole looked worried, but didn't ask any questions. She took him to the lobby, with a few stops in between. People were starting to check out of the hotel, so the elevator was crowded.

Jack crossed the marble floor of the lobby, resisting the urge to play hopscotch in the row of large diamond shapes on its border. He thought it was odd that such childish things could occur to a man his age. He found Reese outside near the cab stand. "Any developments, Reese?"

"Maybe, boss. I finally talked to that cab driver, Esposito. He's out on a fare now. He seems hinky to me. I asked him if he had seen Mrs. Messina on Wednesday, and, of course, he said no, but something was off. Maybe he's just a high-strung guy, but he was jumpy. I think we should keep an eye on him."

"Okay, let's allow him to think he hasn't piqued our interest for the moment. I will talk to him later. In the meantime, head up to Messina's suite. I don't think there will be any action for a while, but I want you there just in case." Fitzgerald handed the ransom note to Reese. "Here's the communication. Pretty bare-bones."

"Are we thinking these aren't the real kidnappers?"

"Or they just got tired of cutting out all those little letters. In any case, stay with him. The guy's pretty shaken. I'll be back soon."

Fitzgerald looked at his watch, as he headed to the hotel's lounge. The area was no longer roped off, but it wasn't very crowded. He took a seat at the same desk he had been using, and started to make a few notes. He had about 20 minutes until Nicole showed up to tell him her news. Jack wondered what she was going to say.

Jack looked up when he heard voices. He saw Nicole entering the lounge area with that bellhop, Kozak. He wasn't pleased.

"Hi, Nicole. I thought you were going to cancel your appointment with your friend."

"We discussed it, Jack, and we thought Philip should come along, as he was with me when I, um, acquired the information, and you might have some questions for him."

Fitzgerald had to admit that was good thinking, but he was still annoyed. He didn't pivot well when plans changed, probably not the best trait for a police detective. "Okay, both of you have a seat. What did you find out, Nicole?"

Nicole proceeded to explain about her visit with Philip to the movie theater and her quick mind-link with the man they called Bogie. She told Jack about the two names she had learned, Lila and Benny, how they seemed to be connected to an image of diamonds, and about the witch's mask.

"I don't know about a Halloween mask," Fitzgerald replied at last, "but we have heard reports of a woman named Lila, who may be running a new gang in town. We don't have a last name, a picture, or even a description. She has been very hard to pin down. There are a couple of Bennys around, so we can look into them. As to the diamonds, well, there are a lot of jewelry stores and merchants. I'll keep this information in mind, but I can't see any connection to the kidnapping here. I shouldn't say this, so keep this between us, but Teddy Messina has received a ransom demand. It may be a straightforward kidnapping for ransom after all, and have nothing to do with you and mistaken identity. Still, I appreciate the information, Nicole."

Nicole looked confused, but stayed silent.

Fitzgerald turned toward Philip. "So, Mr. Kozak, you saw this man too. Anything you can add to Nicole's description?"

"As Nic told you, he looks like Humphrey Bogart, but he is taller. Over 6 feet, I would say. He seemed to know that Nicole was reading him."

"Oh, did he see her?"

"I don't think so. When I saw him looking around, I kissed her. I'm hoping he saw only the back of my head."

"Good thinking." Jack tried to suppress a smirk. "Anything else?"

"Just that I hope this is wrapped up soon for everyone's sake."

"Yes, this is a tough one. Nicole, any more to add?"

"No, that's all I have for now."

"Okay, I know where to find you if I need you. I appreciate your bringing me this new information. Try to stay out of trouble, you two."

"We will, Jack," said Nicole.

"Goodbye, Jack," said Philip.

Fitzgerald glared at that. The "Jack" was for Nicole to use, not Kozak. He wasn't sure he trusted the guy. Jack had always been allergic to pretty boys, especially the young ones. They got away with too much stuff.

He glanced at his watch again, deciding to check the taxi stand in front of the hotel to see if the cab driver Esposito had returned from his fare. Reese's instincts were usually good, and it would be a step in the right direction if they could find out how Mrs. Messina had left the hotel, assuming she had. Jack walked across the marble floor of the lobby once again, and began to chuckle as he crossed the diamond pattern, catching himself. Cops who laughed to themselves tended to be frowned upon.

Stepping out onto Causeway Street, Jack spotted two

cabs at the stand. He tried to effect a casual air, like he was just another guest leaving the hotel, but he knew everything about him screamed "cop." He walked up from behind, and got into the back of the first cab.

The driver turned around and said, "Where to?" Once he saw Jack, the look on Esposito's face said he knew they weren't going anywhere.

"Mr. Esposito, I'm Jack Fitzgerald, Boston Police." The lieutenant flashed his badge. "I'd like to talk to you for a minute. I know you spoke with my man Reese earlier, but we've received some new information, so I just want to ask you a couple of questions."

"I already told him I've never seen that Messina dame."

"I understand, but a couple of new names have come up in our investigation." Jack thought he could use Nicole's information, however questionable, to take a good look at this man, see if Reese's take was on the nose. And maybe he would get some more leads in the bargain. "So, Mr. Esposito, do you know a woman named Lila?"

"Nope, I don't know no woman called Lila."

"What about a man named Benny?"

Fitzgerald watched the cab driver's face, which he could see in the rearview mirror. Esposito flinched, the briefest backward movement of his head, but a dead giveaway. Still Esposito said, "No Benny neither."

"Your face says you do know him."

Esposito opened the door and tried to flee from the cab,

but Fitzgerald nodded to a uniformed officer, who was suddenly at the cab driver's door.

"You're not going anywhere, Esposito. It looks like you do know someone named Benny. Where might we find him?"

"All right, yeah, I know a Benny. What's the big deal?"

"The big deal is that you tried to conceal that fact, and then you tried to run. Any chance Benny asked you to pick up a fare from this hotel?"

"Still no big deal, but yeah, he asked me to pick someone up here."

"Was that someone Mrs. Messina? Here's her photo to refresh your memory."

Esposito grabbed the photo. "Maybe I picked up someone who looked like this. Who knows? I have a lot of fares and I try to keep my eyes on the road."

"That's commendable, but you would remember if you helped to kidnap someone, correct?"

"This is starting to look like a frame-up."

"No frame, but it will go easier on you if you cooperate with us. Kidnapping *is* a big deal. Does your friend Benny have a last name?"

"Probably, but I don't know it."

"How about an address? Give it to us as a sign of good faith."

"All right, all right. I've picked up Benny at a place on Beacon Hill. It's on Phillips Street. I don't remember the house number. Can I go now?"

"I don't think so. You're going to show us the house."
Fitzgerald gestured to the uniformed officer, who opened the
driver's door, and assisted Esposito in exiting the vehicle.
Another officer appeared, as Fitzgerald got out of the cab.
"Officer Wilson is going to park your taxi. Then we are all
going to take a little ride to Phillips Street. Show us where you
picked up Benny, and if your information proves useful, we'll
see if we can help you out of this jam. In the meantime, you
will have to enjoy our hospitality at the Joy Street Police
Station."

"You don't want to mess with Lila, believe me. Now let
me go."

"Oh, so you do know someone named Lila. Thanks for
your cooperation."

Esposito groaned.

As the four men took the short ride to Phillips Street on
Beacon Hill, Fitzgerald marveled at the continued usefulness of
Nicole's information.

Chapter 10

Unmasked

"Virtue has a veil, vice a mask."

— Victor Hugo

P at Messina awoke to another morning of captivity. She had slept a little better on the second night. Her hands were bound in front of her now, and she had lost the restraints on her ankles. The witch had been true to her word, and had given her rewards, as Pat had cooperated. Of course, the door was still locked, and she could see bars on the windows through the shades, so she wasn't going anywhere, but the additional comfort had allowed Pat to rest more easily. She wondered who this woman in the witch's mask was, snatching her forcibly, but still concerned about her well-being.

As if on cue, the witch entered the room. She was alone this time, without her companion, Popeye. "Good morning, Mrs. Messina. I have hopes that we will be able to conclude our business soon. I have contacted your husband, and the next step will be to visit a local phone booth to set up the ransom drop."

Pat allowed herself to feel a little more hope. Maybe this

nightmare would be over soon.

"Assuming your husband can gather the necessary funds, and doesn't allow the police to get in the way, maybe you will be able to go home tomorrow."

Doubt started to creep into Pat's mind at those words. *Don't the police usually foul these things up?* She started to tremble.

"Now, now. Let's have none of that. I have no wish to see you harmed. I'll do my best to make sure the transaction is handled smoothly. I'm not a monster, just a businesswoman. I pride myself on ..."

The witch was interrupted by voices on the street. She rushed to the window and peeked around the shade. "Son of a ..." Her voice trailed off as she caught her mask on the corner of the shade. The elastic string holding the mask in place broke, revealing her face to Pat. "Lila Laroche, at your service." Lila made a dramatic bow.

Pat was speechless.

Lila said, "Sorry, but I must dash." She quickly grabbed the cloth hood from the table and put it over her captive's head.

Pat heard the door slam, as Lila fled the room. She waited for what seemed like an eternity. Suddenly she heard footsteps, shouts, and then a scuffle. It was several more minutes before someone reached her door and crashed through it. Pat was terrified.

"Hello, Mrs. Messina. I assume that is you under the hood. I am Lieutenant Jack Fitzgerald of the Boston police. I'm going to walk over to you now so I can untie you. There's no reason to be afraid. This is over now."

Pat started to cry tears of relief, as she waited to be freed.

Fitzgerald pulled the cloth bag from her head. He looked at her face and said, "It's okay. Let's sit you up, and then I'll untie you."

Pat nodded.

Fitzgerald pulled over the chair and helped Pat to sit down. "Do you think you can answer a couple of questions?"

Pat nodded again.

"We have arrested a man who was wearing a Popeye mask on his head. There is another man who was tied up and had some injuries. Can you tell me about your time here?"

Pat stopped sniffling when she realized the Lieutenant hadn't mentioned a woman. "Did you arrest *her*?"

"Her? Who? We've found no woman here."

"She said her name was Lila."

"Lila was here? When?"

"Not very long ago. She saw you through the window."

"What?" Fitzgerald went to the door. "Wilson, are you back? Get in here!"

Officer Wilson came running.

"Wilson, the woman, Lila, was here when we pulled up. Have you searched the whole place?"

"I am doing that now, but haven't found anyone else. Hargrove has Popeye handcuffed in the car with Esposito. We have called for another car and for an ambulance."

"Good man. Keep looking for the woman. Make sure you check the basement and out back."

"Yes, sir." Wilson disappeared out the door.

"Please tell me, Mrs. Messina, everything you can about this woman. She told you her name?"

"Yes, she said her name was Lila Laroche."

"It's probably a fake, since she volunteered it," Fitzgerald said. "What does she look like?"

"She was wearing a witch's mask until today, when she caught it on the window shade as she was looking out."

The lieutenant raised both eyebrows at that.

Pat continued. "She is colored and has pronounced dimples when she smiles. I'd say she is in her late 30s. That's about all I got in the brief glimpse I had of her face. I saw the rest of her more often. She is tall, 5'8" or so, and dresses quite stylishly."

Fitzgerald made some notes in his book. "We believe she's new to the area, but I will still need you to look at some photos once you've had a chance to recover."

"When can I go back to the hotel and see my husband?"

"Very soon. We have to wait for the other car to arrive. In the meantime, I'd like to ask you a few more questions. Another man was held captive here. Did you hear or see anything related to him?"

"Yes, the witch, I mean, Lila, said he was expecting a shipment of diamonds." Pat wondered if she should mention the mind reading part of the plan. She thought she might appear crazy to the lieutenant, but Lila had intended to kidnap a different person, and the police needed to know that. "The next part may sound strange. Lila thought I was a mind reader, and she wanted me to read that man's mind to find out about the shipment of diamonds."

The lieutenant did not speak for a minute. Pat wondered what he was thinking.

At last Fitzgerald said, "I believe you, Mrs. Messina, but it would be better for the moment if you did not mention this aspect of the case to anyone, even your husband."

"I try not to keep anything from my Teddy."

"I understand, but whether or not mind readers exist, Laroche may try to go after her original target. That may give us an edge in capturing her."

"But I don't see how telling Teddy would matter."

Fitzgerald sighed. "I cannot say much. But there is a woman who stuck her neck out for you. She is the reason we were able to find you today. Please do not tell anyone, including your husband, that Lila thought she had kidnapped a psychic. Your husband did receive a ransom note. Just stick with the ransom story."

Pat was overwhelmed. "All right, I won't say anything about it. Please tell her, whoever she is, thank you from me."

"I will be sure to tell her. Do you know anything about the guy in the Popeye mask?"

"Not much other than he took orders from Lila."

74

"Was there anyone else here working with them?"

"I didn't see anyone else here, although, as you know, they were wearing masks. There was a cab driver involved in the kidnapping. I didn't see much of his face."

"We already have him in custody downstairs."

Pat was losing her concentration. She couldn't stop thinking about the woman who had helped her. At last she said, "I'm so grateful to that woman. I don't know how this would have turned out without her."

"Yes, I'm thankful too. She made this happen."

Suddenly Pat heard a siren. "Is that the car for us?"

"That's the car for the bad guys. I will take you back to the hotel in my car."

Officer Wilson appeared at the doorway. "Excuse me, Sir. The men are here. I can't find the woman anywhere. Should we keep looking?"

"She must have gotten out of here somehow. We'll have to call for more men to continue the search. You and Hargrove will ride with Mrs. Messina and me to the hotel. The other two will take the cab driver and the guy with the mask to the station. Any sign of that ambulance for the other captive?"

Wilson walked to the window and peered around the shade, as Lila had done earlier. "Nothing yet."

"Okay, go sit with the captive. What's his name?"

"Luftman."

"Yeah, stay with Luftman. We'll get underway after the ambulance arrives."

75

Wilson left the room.

"May I use the bathroom before we leave?" Pat asked. "I'm sure I must look a sight."

"Of course, take whatever time you need."

"Is it that bad?"

"Not bad at all."

Pat stood up and felt wobbly.

Fitzgerald lunged to catch her. "I will walk you there," he said.

"Thank you, Lieutenant." Pat held onto Fitzgerald's arm as he walked her down the hallway.

Pat road back to the hotel with Fitzgerald and the two uniformed officers. She had many needs competing for her attention, but at the moment she had just one desire—to see Teddy again. She wasn't sure why she felt nervous. She was finally heading back to her husband, after all. Pat assumed such feelings were normal after all she had been through.

Lieutenant Fitzgerald spoke to his two men, who were seated in the back. "When we arrive at the hotel, I want you to stay outside. Uniforms will call attention to us as we walk through the lobby. I'm hoping Mrs. Messina and I will look like any other couple walking to an elevator, thereby avoiding prying eyes."

"Thank you, Lieutenant, for your consideration." said Pat.

The ride to the hotel was short, and Pat soon found herself entering the lobby on Fitzgerald's arm. They walked toward the elevators, but none were available.

Pat was feeling jittery, and she thought someone might recognize her after the newspaper report Lila had mentioned.

Fitzgerald seemed to pick up on this. He shifted his position in the elevator hallway to give her more coverage. "I should be able to block you from sight with this extra bulk of mine," he said.

An elevator finally arrived. Pat noticed it was operated by the same girl who had taken her down from her suite on the day she had been kidnapped. "Hello, again," she managed to say.

"Hello, Mrs. Messina!" The woman seemed flustered, but delighted.

Fitzgerald put his finger to his lips at the elevator operator's loud proclamation. "A little lower, please, Nicole. We're trying to get upstairs without being noticed. Please take us to the top floor, no stops," said Fitzgerald.

Nicole nodded.

Pat wondered why the lieutenant knew the elevator operator's first name, but figured he had been spending some time at the hotel since the kidnapping. The ride to the top was fast and somehow soothing, a note of normalcy in a week that had been anything but usual. When they reached their destination, Pat noticed how the woman, Nicole, used the controls to align the elevator with the floor.

Nicole said, "watch your step," even though she had done the job perfectly.

Pat and Fitzgerald stepped into the hallway. Fitzgerald turned to Nicole and said, "I'll talk to you in a few minutes."

Pat's curiosity was piqued even further, but she started to search for the room key in her purse. Lila had been kind enough to leave her the key, although the witch had helped herself to the cash in the purse. Pat didn't need the key, however, as Teddy was already opening the door to the suite. Pat's husband took her hand and gently pulled her into his arms.

Fitzgerald waited a minute, and then said, "Look, you two, I'm going to leave you alone for a while, but I've got to come back and ask Mrs. Messina more questions. I'm heading to the station, and I'll be back in about an hour. I know that's not enough time, but that's all I can give you."

Pat turned around, and reached for Fitzgerald's hand. "Thank you for rescuing me, Lieutenant."

Teddy said, "Yes, thank you. I don't know how to repay you."

"No need to thank me. I'm just glad this story has a happy ending."

Chapter 11

Secrets of Beacon Hill

"We are not makers of history. We are made by history."

— Martin Luther King, Jr.

L ila Laroche left her witch's mask and Mrs. Messina behind, as she fled the room. She had spotted police uniforms, even with the obstructed view from the basement apartment, and knew it was time to run. Lila realized she was abandoning Benny to the police, but he was a necessary sacrifice. A lady had to leave herself options, after all.

She opened a closet in the hallway and stepped inside. The door made a loud creak when she closed it, and Lila winced. She hoped Mrs. Messina hadn't heard it. Grabbing a flashlight from the shelf and pushing a couple of jackets aside, Lila located the three coat hooks on the side wall. She gave the left hook a tug, and then the right one. There was a sound like tumblers falling into place, and the back wall of the closet popped open. Stepping onto the landing on the other side, Lila turned and pushed the closet's secret panel until it closed with a *snap*. She started down the stairs, which led directly to the sub-basement.

Lila had learned all the secrets this building possessed while visiting every summer from Tupelo. Her grandmother had told her stories of the Underground Railroad, and how there had been a safe house on this very street with a tunnel underneath it. Escaped slaves from the South had been able to find refuge in Boston, but bounty hunters searched for them there. During her childhood explorations, Lila had found the hidden tunnel Nan had described. It was in the sub-basement, and had provided an escape route for the hunted when needed. She was heading there now.

Once Lila reached the lower level, she quickly assessed her options. She could hide in the sub-basement, but the area could also be accessed from the regular basement above, so it wasn't a secure hiding place. An alternate plan would bring her to street level, where she could leave the neighborhood behind, but she would look conspicuous after her dirty crawl through the tunnel. If the cops commenced an immediate search for her, they might find her on the street. But she had a third choice, a daring one. She could double back to Phillips Street and use another of her secret weapons. To do this, she would have to step briefly onto the same street where the police presence was. She decided it was worth the risk.

Lila dragged a stout, worm-eaten cabinet aside, and entered the tunnel. There was no way she could move the furniture back into place once inside and facing away, so she would have to leave the opening uncovered. A furnace several feet from the opening provided some coverage, but a thorough search would reveal her escape route. She hoped the cops wouldn't find their way to the sub-basement, at least for a while. The tunnel was only 4-feet wide and not even as high, so she had to crawl, a fun adventure for a 10-year-old girl, but an indignity for a grown woman, especially one in a nice suit. *Needs must*, Lila thought.

As she crawled through the tunnel, Lila briefly considered that she might be getting too old for this line of work. *A thought for another time*, she concluded. She remembered her Nan's history lessons, about the African Meeting House and abolitionists on Beacon Hill, but hadn't paid much attention until Nan mentioned the secret tunnel. Now she was using her elbows to drag herself forward in that very tunnel. Nan probably hadn't envisioned that her information would be used in such a way.

Lila finally reached the tunnel's exit. It ended in another sub-basement on West Cedar Street. On this end, there was an old standing mirror covering the tunnel's opening, and she used her arms to push it aside. At that point, her hands fell on the dirt floor, and Lila placed one hand in front of the other, trying to pull herself out of the tunnel. Eventually one knee crashed to the floor, and then the other. *That's going to hurt tomorrow*, she thought.

Dusting herself off as best she could, Lila walked up one flight to the regular basement and took more stairs up to a closed door. She opened it and peered into a hallway. The coast was clear, so she moved hastily through the hallway and out the back door into an alley.

Now she had to be brave. She needed to exit the alley, turn right, and walk with confidence down Phillips Street. Nothing amiss, nothing to see here. Lila brushed herself down one more time, took a deep breath, and turned onto the street. She could see that the unmarked police car was still there with two men seated in the back. One of them was certainly Benny, no doubt handcuffed and probably still wearing his Popeye mask. Poor Benny. But she couldn't see any uniforms on the street. She took about 15 steps, and then took three more up the stairs into a different row house, where she had a second residence. This was Lila's own apartment, but not under the name Laroche. She doubted the police would look for her here, and Benny didn't know about it. No one knew, except Gerard St. Cloud, whose name was on the lease. The other place was actually Nan's apartment. Nan was in a nursing home now, but Lila was keeping up with the rent.

Yes, it was nice to have options. Lila hoped she never ran out of them.

Chapter 12

A Visit to Phillips Street

"Everything in this world has a hidden meaning."

— Nikos Kazantzakis

The panel on Nicole's elevator lit up, indicating that someone was calling for service from the 17th floor. She assumed it was Fitzgerald, and took the elevator straight to the top. When she opened the accordion gates and glass doors, Jack was standing there.

"Hi, Nicole. I'd like to talk to you for a minute downstairs."

Nicole suppressed a sigh. She had been hoping that the reappearance of Pat Messina signaled the end of Jack's need for her mind reading abilities. But he wanted to talk to her again, and the look on his face said that it wasn't just to say thank you. Jack looked like a man with a lot on his mind.

"Okay, I can give you a minute, but then I'll have to get back to work."

Jack nodded.

When they reached the lobby, Nicole placed her elevator temporarily out of service. Sally, the girl in the other elevator assigned to floors 10-17, would have to pick up the slack. Nicole and Jack sat on a long, low bench just around the corner from the elevator bank.

Jack said, "Please don't worry about getting in trouble with your boss. I have already told him how much help you have been to me on the case."

"But you haven't mentioned ..."

"Of course not," Jack interrupted. "I told him you have filled in as my stenographer after work, so we wouldn't have to inconvenience Mr. Messina at this difficult time or call in a stenographer from the station."

"Hey, you're pretty good at this."

"I'll take that as a compliment. Anyway, I'd like you to do the stenographer bit again for me, this time with Pat. Not that I doubt her honesty, but things might not be clear in her mind after all she's been through. We can do it later this afternoon. You'll have to take some time off of work, but I will clear it with Altman. I have to go back to the station for about an hour, but we can do it after that. Are you willing?"

"I will do it to help Pat."

"Thank you. And thank you from Pat. Although she doesn't know the identity of the ...," he lowered his voice, "... mind reader, she wanted to make sure I gave that person her thanks. She was overwhelmed that someone stepped up to help her like that."

Nicole fought back some tears, but managed to ask, "How did she know a mind reader was involved?"

"You were absolutely right about the reason for the kidnapping. The kidnapper, Lila—and you were right about that name too—told Pat why she was there—to read someone's mind! Your information really broke this case."

Nicole felt a surge of pride. Although her mind reading had caused some of these problems in the first place, it was also providing some solutions. "And do you have this Lila in custody?"

Jack suddenly looked embarrassed. "I'm afraid not. We have the cab driver and Lila's other accomplice, Benny, in custody, but she escaped."

A shiver of fear went through Nicole. Lila was still at large, and Nicole had been her original target. "Jack, am I safe with this woman on the loose?"

"I think her likely play will be to flee the area. Her men are under arrest and we know where her headquarters are. At minimum, she will find a place to lie low. She's not going to call attention to herself."

"That's a relief."

"I'll go talk to Altman, and then I'll head back to the station. I'll meet you around 3 PM. Okay?"

"Yes, but Philip is not going to like this."

"Kozak will get over it."

Nicole met Philip for their afternoon break as usual. He had barely sat down, when she said, "Have you heard? Pat

Messina is safe and back with Teddy!"

"What? That's wonderful news!"

Nicole lowered her voice. "Jack told me that my information broke the case! My theory about the kidnapping was correct, and even the name Lila was right. She is the ringleader!"

"A woman?"

"Yes, Philip, a woman! And she has escaped! Fitzgerald needs my help to read Pat, in case she has some clues about Lila, but doesn't realize it."

"Wow! Will this ever end?"

"I know it's dragging on, but I certainly will be better off if they catch Lila, so I think I should help."

"I can't wait until this is behind us. Speaking of us, I have a day off next Saturday. It would be nice if we could go out on a Saturday date like a normal couple. Can we finally bring this relationship out into the open?"

"I'm sorry, honey, but I can't tell my parents right now. If my mind reading ability somehow comes out, that will be enough of a shock."

"I can see that. Boy, I wish I had never asked you for that favor."

"What's done is done. We have to move forward now. I will tell my parents when this is all over, I promise. In the meantime, I am going to confide in my sister. I think Maria will be willing to cover for me next Saturday. She and I can act like we are going out together, and then Maria can do whatever she wants. I don't like hiding things from my parents, but I don't see any other option right now. I will ask Maria tonight. I know this isn't as much as you wanted, but it is a step in the right direction."

Philip smiled. "A definite step in the right direction. I don't like hiding our love away. We aren't doing anything wrong."

Nicole tried not to look startled. Philip had never used the "L" word before. Were they truly in love? It seemed a little soon, but maybe they were heading in that direction. Finally she said, "I want things out in the open too, but my parents have their old ways, and I need to take this gradually. They still don't speak much English, which will be another issue when you meet them, unless, of course, you speak *Abruzzese.*

"What's that? I thought they were Italian."

"It's the dialect spoken in the part of Italy they came from."

"And you speak it?"

"Of course, but I have never learned to read it. Do your parents speak Ukrainian at home?"

"No, they speak English. They want us to be American."

"My parents aren't as modern as that. I will ask my sister tonight about covering for us next Saturday. That means someone in my family will know, so I hope that will make you feel better about this."

"It does." Philip winked at her.

"Philip, you are such a flirt." Nicole giggled. Glancing at her watch, she said, "I'd better get back to work. Then I have to meet Fitzgerald at 3 PM. He said he would clear it with Mr. Altman. He also said he is putting in a good word for me, so maybe something positive will come of this after all."

"I hope so," Philip said.

Nicole took her elevator out of service at 3 PM, and waited for Fitzgerald in the lobby. She sat on a love seat facing the door, and pretended she was a swanky hotel guest. She wondered whether she would ever be able to stay in such a fine hotel herself.

Jack walked through the door about 10 minutes after 3 PM. "Hello, Nicole," he said. "Sorry I'm late. Let's head upstairs."

"You remembered to clear this with Mr. Altman, right?"

"Right. You're all clear."

Nicole unlocked her elevator, and the two took the quick trip to the 17th floor once again.

Outside Messina's suite, Jack said, "Here's a steno pad. Just do what you did last time, but focus on Pat. I'm particularly interested in things you read that she doesn't say out loud."

"No offense, Jack, but I'm hoping this is the last reading I will have to do for you."

"Oh, was Kozak upset?"

"Very funny. I'm sure you can understand that we would both like to put this behind us."

"Yes, I understand. You've been great, and you know I appreciate it. Sorry to bug you about Kozak. He's just a bit too 'dreamy' for me. That's the word you kids use, isn't it?"

She laughed. "Yes, you're using the word correctly. Philip is a 'dreamboat.' But he's also a good guy."

"He got you into this, didn't he?"

"He did, and he has apologized several times. He just wanted to move up a bit in the world. There's nothing wrong with that, is there?"

"I suppose not, but pretty boys tend to rely on their looks to get favors. You should ..."

The door to Messina's suite suddenly opened, and Teddy said, "I thought I heard voices. Come on in."

"Thanks," said Fitzgerald. "And you remember, Miss Rossi. She is helping us again today."

"Hello, Miss Rossi. It's nice to see you, especially under these improved circumstances."

"Yes, Mr. Messina. I was so happy to hear your news."

"Pat, Lieutenant Fitzgerald is here with his stenographer, Miss Rossi."

Pat was lounging on the sofa, and looked up at the visitors. "Hello. Oh, I've already met ... Miss Rossi, but I thought she was the elevator operator."

Sneaking a quick glance at his stenographer, Fitzgerald said, "She is one of the elevator operators, but Nicole has been helping me so that we don't have to question you both at the station."

"That's very considerate," said Pat. She nodded at Nicole. "Please sit down, both of you."

Everyone found a chair, and Fitzgerald got down to business. "I will try to make this as brief as possible. We did search our files for the name Lila Laroche, but, as I expected, we didn't find anything. I'm sure it's an alias. I do have some photos for you to examine. I know you saw her face only briefly, but please give them a look." He handed the photos to Pat.

Mrs. Messina inspected each photo, finally declaring, "None of these women look like Lila to me."

Nicole was scratching away at her steno pad, while trying to read Pat's mind. It definitely broke her concentration to perform the stenography act, and what she was writing was mostly gibberish, but she was managing to break through to Pat's thoughts.

"Have you remembered anything else, Mrs. Messina?" Fitzgerald asked. "For example, how did Laroche talk? Did she seem educated? Have an accent?"

"Yes, she spoke like an educated woman. Oh, did I mention that she had a Southern drawl?"

"Good to know," said Fitzgerald. "Could you detect any particular region?"

"Region? Sorry, I'm rather bad at that."

"That's all right. It confirms our theory that she is

probably new to the area, and we can rule out the northeastern states as the region where she was raised. Anything else?" Jack asked.

"I don't think so. As I mentioned, she was pretty much covered up, wig, mask, suit with slacks, and even gloves."

"How about when she left the last time?"

"Well, I was lying on a mattress in the corner with a bag over my head. I heard her walk to the door and close it. I didn't hear her talk to anyone."

As Nicole read Pat's mind, she picked up a sound, a distant creaking noise, most likely from a door, but not the door Lila had used to exit the room. It was probably nothing, but she would mention it to Jack. In the meantime, Pat's eyes had started to well up with tears.

Bounding up and placing his hand on Pat's shoulder, Teddy said, "Lieutenant, my wife has been through a lot. She has examined your photos. Can we wrap this up? She does need to rest."

"Of course, Mr. Messina. I'm sorry to dredge up these memories for your wife, but we do want to catch the woman who calls herself Lila Laroche so she can't do this to anyone again." Jack turned toward Pat. "I'm sorry to put you through this, Mrs. Messina. I think that's all I need for now. I'll let you rest and be in touch tomorrow if I have any further questions."

"Thank you, Lieutenant. I am so grateful that you rescued me. Thank you too, Miss Rossi ... Nicole. I'm glad you were available so I didn't have to go to the police station."

Everyone said their goodbyes, and Nicole and Jack exited the suite. When they were in the hallway, Jack said, "Let's talk in the lobby."

Nicole hadn't gained any information other than the door creak, so she thought this might be the end of her time with Jack Fitzgerald. Pat Messina was home, so to speak, the police had suspects in custody, and Jack was in possession of at least a few leads on the woman known as Lila Laroche. Maybe she and Philip could move on with their lives now.

After they found a seat in the lobby, Jack asked, "Did you get anything?"

Nicole explained about the creaking noise, and Jack said, "Is that it?"

"Yes, Jack, that's it."

"I was hoping for more. Would it help if you went to the location?"

"Jack!"

A few heads snapped in her direction. Nicole hadn't meant to speak so loudly. "Sorry," she said in a lower voice. "I want to help, but I don't work for you."

"You want to get Lila off the street, don't you?"

"I said I would help because I felt responsible for what happened to Pat, but she is back with Teddy now. I'd like to go back to my normal life too."

"I understand. I might be able to get you some money as a confidential informant. Would that help?"

"That would be nice, but it's not about that. It's about

putting this behind me and moving on. I made a mistake. I shouldn't have done the favor for Philip. He knows it and I know it. We want this to be over."

"But Lila does have vital information about you. She doesn't know your identity yet, at least as far as I'm aware, but she does know there is a mind reader connected to this hotel and that the woman looks like Pat Messina. You will be safer when she is behind bars."

"First you told me I'm safe, and now you're saying I'm not."

"Well, I'm not a psychic like you. I'm hoping that she has fled the area. That's what most criminals do when they're hot, but I can't possibly know for sure."

"Oh, Jack, how did this all get so complicated?"

"I know. You're a fine young woman, Nicole, and I'm sorry one lapse in judgment led to so much trouble. I do think, though, that your help will be key in finding Laroche and bringing this episode to its best conclusion."

"All right, Jack. How do you think I can help?"

"I'd like to know more about your special abilities. Can you read objects by holding them? I'm not sure if that's the right way to put it, but I think you know what I mean. Get impressions from them?"

"I'd like to know more about my special abilities too, Jack. My mother put a lot of fear in me about using them, so I haven't had a chance to conduct many experiments. I have tried a few times to read objects, but I haven't gotten anything from them. My power does seem to be increasing as I use it, though, so it's possible additional abilities will surface later. My mother told me that some of the women before her even had the power to mesmerize, but I haven't seen anything like that yet. It's hard to know what lesson I'm supposed to be learning here. Using my power caused all this trouble in the first place, but using it has been helping too. What if I cause some other problem without realizing it?"

"Maybe the best way to look at it is you are trying to finish what you started. If you can help me find Lila and get her behind bars, then that will close the book on this case. After that, you, and only you, can decide how, when, and if you want to use your abilities."

"That makes sense, Jack. Thanks."

"So, are you willing to go to Lila's with me? We can do it after you finish work. It's on Beacon Hill, so it shouldn't take very long. We can try to identify that creaking door you heard, and maybe you can pick up a few objects to see if you get anything from them. I will drive you home after that."

Nicole said, "Okay," but she was still reluctant.

Fitzgerald looked at his watch. "I'll meet you back here a little after 4 PM. Don't look so glum, Nicole. Maybe we'll find something that will wrap this right up."

"Maybe," she said, but she was just humoring Jack.

Nicole found herself in Lila Laroche's apartment on

Beacon Hill. It was a normal home in some respects. Parts of it, like the living room, looked like someone had lived there for a long time, but others, like the room where Pat was kept, were very sparse. Nicole did not like being in that room at all.

"I know this isn't pleasant for you, Nicole. Let's just try a couple of things," Fitzgerald said. He picked up a witch's mask and handed it to Nicole. "This is the mask Laroche wore. See if you can get anything from it."

Nicole looked the mask over, and tried to stare into the eyes that weren't there. Nothing came through—a blank, just like the eyes. "Sorry, Jack, I'm not getting anything."

"Why don't you try sitting in the chair. Maybe that will help you see things from Pat's perspective."

The thought of sitting in Pat's chair made Nicole feel queasy, but she seated herself. She looked around the room, at the drawn shades, the mattress on the floor, the lamp on the table, the door that had separated Pat from the outside world, and Nicole read nothing, except panic and sadness. "I'm sorry, Jack, but this doesn't seem to be working. When can we leave?"

"Let's try all the doors and see if we can identify the creak you told me about. After that, we can go."

Nicole couldn't help but notice that Jack was taking her readings more seriously now. They walked out of the room, and Jack opened a door in the hallway. It was a closet, not an exit, and Jack started to close the door. Suddenly the door made the loud creaking noise that Nicole had sensed. "That's it, Jack, the sound I heard, when I was reading Pat."

Jack opened the door once again. He stepped inside and looked everything over twice. "It's a closet. She probably just grabbed a jacket. I guess this was a wasted trip after all. I will take you home." Closing the closet door, Jack said, "I know we didn't get anything out of this visit, but I want you to know how much your help has meant to this investigation. Your information helped us to bring Pat Messina safely home. It's hard to be an unsung hero, and I wish I could sing your praises from the rooftop, but we both know that's not a good idea. I want to try to help you, though, so I'm going to talk to your supervisor again. Maybe that will get you a raise or a promotion."

"Thank you, Jack. I have so many mixed feelings about everything that's happened, but it's nice to know something good came out of using my gift, if you can call it that."

"I think it is fair to call it a gift."

Nicole smiled.

The two left the apartment and walked up the few stairs to street level. "So, any plans on this Friday night?" Jack asked.

"Nothing special. I'm planning to stay home and relax. Maybe I'll play checkers with my sister. Exciting, huh?"

"Well, I'm going back to work on reports at the station, so your plans don't sound bad."

"Won't your son be waiting for you?"

"No, he lives with his mother. She and I divorced a few years ago."

"I'm sorry, Jack."

"It's okay. I still get to see him. They live in Cambridge, so he's not very far away. Jimmy's a great kid."

"I'm sure he is."

Nicole felt a sudden distraction as she stood on the brick sidewalk of Phillips Street. Her eyes were drawn to a row house a couple of doors down the block.

"Everything okay?" Jack asked. "You suddenly look miles away."

"Not that far away, Jack. Not that far at all."

Chapter 13

A Time to Run

"When you're acting, you're escaping
and hiding behind something."

— Tamsin Egerton

Lila Laroche peered out from the crack between the window and the shade. It was getting close to sunset, but there was still enough light to see the street clearly. The unmarked car she had spotted earlier had returned and was now parked in front of Nan's apartment. A man and a woman were conversing on the sidewalk near the car. The tall, husky man looked like a cop, probably a detective, and the woman ... the woman! Was that the mind reader? She resembled Pat Messina, with her trim figure and dark, wavy hair at shoulder length, reminding Lila of the mistaken identity that had come to haunt her. Was the mind reader working with the cops? *That girl has been nothing but trouble*, Lila thought.

Laroche backed away from the window. She figured the woman couldn't read minds from that distance, but there was no point in being conspicuous. She waited about five minutes and then peeked out again. The car was gone. *Whew!* The presence of the mentalist was troubling, but Lila's strategy of doubling back to her own apartment had worked. Still, she wanted to be ready for anything, and figured it was best to get dressed after her shower. She slipped off her robe, changing into a dress "Lila" would never wear: polka dots, lace collar, loose-fitting, and taken from Nan's closet. She pulled her hair back into a severe bun, applied no makeup to her face, and added an ugly brooch as her only jewelry to complete her dowdy look. No master criminals here, just a genteel, old-fashioned girl.

About an hour later, after Lila had consumed a small snack, there was a light tap on her door. Lila ran to the window, but saw neither a police vehicle nor the detective's unmarked car. She walked to the door and looked through the peephole, recognizing her building manager, Mr. Jacoby.

Lila opened the door, but didn't unchain it. "Yes?"

"Oh, Miss St. Cloud, may I speak with you for a moment?"

"I'm expecting company, Mr. Jacoby. What's this about?"

"It will take just a moment of your time. I need to inform you about something happening in the building."

"Very well. What is it?"

"May I come in for a few minutes?"

"As I said, I'm rather busy. Can't you tell me right here?"

Suddenly the husky fellow Lila had seen from her

window stepped out from his hiding place. She quickly slammed the door in his face, bolting the lock. As she ran toward the bedroom, Lila could hear bangs, groans, and curses as the man tried to break down the door.

Lila stepped into her bedroom closet and shut the door behind her, locking it. She pulled a chain above her head to turn on the light. Grabbing one of Nan's coats to match her dress, an already packed overnight case, and her pocketbook, Lila turned toward the side wall. There were three coat hooks on the wall, as there had been in Nan's closet. The combination here, however, was different. She gave the right hook a tug, and then the left one. Hidden tumblers shifted into position here as well, and the back wall of the closet popped open. Lila closed the panel and walked quietly down the stairs. There was an exit from the regular basement in this house, so no need to crawl through a tunnel, but she did run the risk of encountering someone in this space, which was accessible to everyone in the row house. She'd have to take that chance.

There were no options left for Lila on Beacon Hill at the moment. She had only one choice now—to run, well, walk—out of there, posing as a genteel lady. She would stroll across Boston Common and down to Winter Street, where she would catch an MTA train to Egleston Square. Lila would call her cousin from a phone booth and hope she was home. This was all that was left, the last option, at least for the time being.

Lila remained alert during her walk through the common. No one seemed to be following her. She boarded the train to Forest Hills, and managed to find a seat in the middle section. Looking around at the faces of her fellow passengers, she saw that no one was paying her one bit of attention. *Good,* she thought. She let her guard down just a little, and started to think. *How did he find me? Was it Benny? I thought Benny didn't know about my other place. What about Jacoby? Did he spot me when I looked disheveled after coming through the tunnel? That wouldn't have been enough to call the cops about. And the mind reader! From everything I've heard, they need to be in the same room with the subject, and as close as possible. Where did I go wrong?*

The stops rolled by as the train left the tunnels of downtown Boston and moved through the neighborhoods on an elevated line. It was dark now, so there wasn't much for Lila to see out the window. She searched for some change in her pocketbook so she could make her call from the phone booth, once she arrived at the station.

At last she reached the Egleston Square stop. Lila walked down the stairs from the elevated platform and located a phone booth on the lower level. Inserting a nickel into the phone, she dialed her cousin Regina Preston in Mattapan. Regina answered on two rings. *Thank goodness,* Lila thought.

"Hi, Reggie. This is Ruby. Sorry to bother you at such short notice, but I'm having a horrendous problem with mice at my apartment. The exterminator is coming in a couple of days, but I can't stand one more night of it. Can I stay with you?"

"Sorry to hear that, Ruby. We have no plans for tonight, so you are welcome to stay here. When can I expect you?"

"I am at Egleston now. As long as it takes for the streetcar to get me there."

"Goodness! That soon? I need to clean this place."

"Don't worry, Reggie. You know I'm not fussy."

"All right, but don't bring your white glove, and you'll have to take potluck for supper."

"Sounds perfect! I will see you and Earl soon."

"Okay, but don't rush." Regina laughed.

"I will walk slowly from the streetcar stop. Bye!" Lila hung up the phone. She located the trolley for Mattapan, and boarded the car. On the ride past Franklin Park, Lila reviewed the lies, er, story—lie was such a nasty word—that she had told cousin Regina about her life. Reggie thought her cousin Ruby worked as a telephone operator, a respectable job, but not very glamorous. Ruby had a stern boss, Mr. Taylor, who picked on her a lot. Ruby thought he didn't like colored girls, but she had to stay because she needed the work right now. She had a boyfriend, Benny, but they had just broken up. That last bit would be new information to Regina. The rest Lila could improvise.

Lila clutched her overnight bag and pocketbook, as the streetcar turned onto Blue Hill Avenue. Her small cases and their contents were not much to work with, but Lila had been in worse shape than this. New options would materialize, they always did. Still, she couldn't keep herself from feeling a little sad. She would have to shake it off before she reached cousin Regina's house. *Onward, girl.*

Chapter 14

Locked Doors

"Sometimes we stare so long at a door that is closing
that we see too late the one that is open."
— Alexander Graham Bell

"Jacoby, where's that key? I need to open this door!"
Fitzgerald yelled.

The building manager fumbled with his keys, looking
for the master. Finding it at last, he started to insert it into the
doorknob, but Fitzgerald grabbed it. "Let me," the detective
said. "Please stand away from the door." Fitzgerald inserted the
key into the doorknob, and turned the lock. "Okay, now the
second key," Jack said.

"Second key?" Mr. Jacoby looked at the door. "Oh, she
must have installed her own deadbolt. Tenants are not
supposed to do that without permission."

"Does this apartment have a back door?" Jack asked.

"No, this is the only one."

"Mr. Jacoby, you can go now," Jack said. "Thanks for your help."

"Please don't break down the door!" Jacoby exclaimed.

"You can send us the bill for any damages."

The manager walked away in a sulk.

Fitzgerald took a few steps away from the door, and threw his body against it. "Ow!" He walked around in a circle, rubbing his right shoulder. Next he tried using his foot to break down the door. That effort also met with no success. *This looks much easier in the movies*, Jack thought.

Officers Wilson and Hargrove arrived in the nick of time to lend their shoulders to the effort. Jack was relieved to have some younger bodies on the scene. He had once been like them, new and full of fire, but he was middle-aged now, his flames dampened by years on the job. He backed off and gave way to the force of youth. They broke down the door in no time.

With their revolvers drawn, the three men set about searching Lila's apartment. "Miss Laroche? This is Jack Fitzgerald, Boston police. Please come quietly. There's no place to hide."

Laroche did not answer.

"She must be here somewhere," Hargrove said.

Jack moved into the bedroom, and found what he assumed to be a closet. "Come out, Miss Laroche ... Lila. It's all over now," he told the door.

Still nothing.

Jack grabbed the door handle, jiggling it, but it was locked. *Who locks a closet?* "Wilson, Hargrove, get in here!"

Both men came running.

"What's happening out there?"

"Not a thing," said Wilson. "It's not a very big drop from those front windows, but they are locked. I don't see how she could have gotten out that way and then locked a window from the sidewalk."

"This closet is locked too," said Fitzgerald. "Damn suspicious. Jacoby said there was no other exit. Hargrove, run down to the car and get a crowbar."

Hargrove scurried off, and the two remaining men kept watch. Wilson looked under the bed, while Jack guarded the closet door. "Imagine!" Fitzgerald said, "She had a second apartment right here on the same block. Pretty brazen to stay in the neighborhood." Jack thought Lila was bad to the bone, but he was starting to admire her cunning and bravery. "According to Jacoby, the name on the lease is Gerard St. Cloud. He says Lila is Gerard's sister, but Jacoby knows her only as Miss St. Cloud. He couldn't verify her first name. We'll have to check out those names, but I'm betting they're phonies. I wonder how the brother fits in the picture. Lila is clearly the gang leader."

"How did you find her, Sir?" Wilson asked.

"I had a tip from an informant."

Hargrove returned with the crowbar. Jack had learned his lesson earlier, so he let the two uniformed officers handle the door-busting operation. At this point, he sincerely doubted that Lila was in the closet, but he had his revolver ready anyway. The men finally got the door open, and Jack peered into the space. It was a closet. He wasn't sure what he was expecting, but he had convinced himself it couldn't be just that. Where had Lila gone? Was she some sort of magician? A witch? Maybe she had chosen that mask for a reason.

"She's not here, men. I don't know how she got out of this apartment. You two check the nearby streets. I'm going to look around a little more."

The light was still on in the closet, but Jack took out his flashlight for a better view. He looked at the ceiling to see if there was some sort of hatch up there. *Nothing.* He touched all the walls, but they seemed solid. *What am I missing here?* Then he remembered the closet at Lila's other apartment. Pat Messina had heard the noise of the closet closing, as reported by Nicole, but not the sound of Lila's footsteps retreating down the hallway. Was he dealing with some sort of secret passageways? Fitzgerald started searching for buttons or latches. He spotted the coat hooks on the side wall and began to tug at them. Nothing happened when he pulled the one on the left. He tried the center one with the same result. *This has got to be the one,* he thought, tugging on the right hook. It pulled away from the wall in a downward arc, and locked in that position, but there was no *alakazam* moment, no sudden appearance of a doorway. *Crap.* Fitzgerald looked around, but didn't see any other hooks or levers except the ones he had already tried. He decided to pull on the middle hook again, but no luck. *Well, there's not much to lose,* he thought, so he tugged on the left hook, and the back wall of the closet opened.

"Eureka!" Jack yelled. He stepped through the opening onto a small landing, and saw a narrow staircase leading down, presumably to a basement. *So this is how she did it.* He pointed his flashlight toward the staircase, and started taking the steps down to the next level. Was she hiding down there or was there an exit? Jack followed the stairs to the bottom, opened the door, and found himself behind a large breakfront, no doubt meant to obscure the hidden staircase. He stepped out from behind it, realizing he was in an enclosed storage room, which contained other pieces of furniture and some boxes. Perhaps the apartment, the storage room, and even the entire house had been in Lila's family for decades. Bootleggers had been known to create secret passages during Prohibition. Maybe her family had been involved in that. Jack would have Wilson and Hargrove search this room for clues later. Maybe there would be some scrap of evidence that would lead them to Lila Laroche.

Fitzgerald emerged from the storage room into the shared basement. He saw a door, and he knew it had been Laroche's means of escape. Or should he say, "St. Cloud's"? Whatever her name was, it had taken him too long to get here. She was gone.

✳ ✳ ✳

"Get Benny Bingham into interrogation now!" Fitzgerald bellowed. He was in no mood for delays. Lila Laroche had escaped right under his nose, and it was an embarrassment for a man of his experience, secret passages or not. Bingham hadn't betrayed Lila during his first interview, but Fitzgerald had more information he could use against him now. Laroche was gone, but Benny Bingham, Lila's partner, henchman, boyfriend ... whatever he was, might know about her possible hideouts or relatives.

Entering the dimly lit interrogation room, Fitzgerald said, "Good evening, Mr. Bingham ... Benny. I have a few more questions to ask." Fitzgerald seated himself at a scarred metal table, facing the prisoner. "We found your girlfriend's second apartment today. You were loyal, and kept quiet about it, but we know where it is now. No sense in holding back."

"What second apartment? Lila didn't have a second apartment. She would have told me."

"But she did have one, just a couple of doors down from the one you where you two stayed together on Phillips Street. Your girlfriend didn't tell you about her other place? Not very nice."

"I didn't know anything about it, and she's not my girlfriend. I could never be good enough for a woman like Lila."

"Touching, Benny, very touching."

Benny started squirming in his seat. He had light hair and a fair complexion, and should have been handsome, but somehow his coloring didn't match his features. "Where is she? Where is Lila? Do you have her?"

"Unfortunately we do not. If you tell us where she is, we can bring her here."

"I will never tell you."

"I think you don't know where your girlfriend is, Mr. Bingham."

Benny suddenly looked very sad. "All right, I know."

Fitzgerald leaned forward. "Where is she?"

"She is in a palace in Shangri-La, where she will live for many hundreds of years. You will never find her, and she will still be here when your grandchildren are gone."

"Get him out of here!" Fitzgerald yelled. Shangri-La? Was Benny being a wise guy or was there something wrong with him? Maybe Bingham had seen *Lost Horizon* too many times. Mind reading, secret tunnels and Shangri-La. What kind of case was this?

Chapter 15

Waiting for Maria

"There are no secrets that time does not reveal."

— Jean Racine

Nicole was stretched out on her bed, listening to the radio. She kept the volume low, because her mother was sensitive to the noise. Her mother also didn't like her to rest on top of the bedspread, but Nicole was tired, so she had given in to her immediate need. She was waiting for her sister, Maria, to get out of the bathroom, so they could discuss her secret plan for seeing Philip a week from Saturday. Nicole was going to spill the beans about her relationship with Philip, so she was trying to decide how much to reveal. Not that there was much to tell, but their relationship was moving forward, and Philip had used the word "love." It was time to share the news with someone in the family, and that someone was Maria.

Perry Como's hit song "Some Enchanted Evening" came on the radio. Nicole loved Perry, and not just because his parents had come from Abruzzi, just like hers. His voice somehow sounded like home to her and the people she knew. She moved closer to the radio to hear Perry's voice better. Her

Philco Transitone model reminded her a little of a cockroach, with its hard shell and brownish red color, but she had bought it with her own money, so it was special to her.

Teddy Messina's latest song followed Perry's. It was a romantic ballad, and Nicole liked the sound of it. She smiled, thinking of Teddy and Pat, and what a lovely couple they made. Then her thoughts turned to Philip again, and what their future might hold. Some commercials interrupted the flow of her thoughts. The jolt made Nicole remember her mission. *Where is Maria? She sure is taking her time.*

When the music returned, Nicole pursued a new line of thought. She was starting to learn more about her special abilities in regard to distance. Nicole had been able to read Lila's thoughts from several doors down the street. And they had come to her—she hadn't gone looking for them. Was that because Nicole's power was increasing or because Lila was sending so loudly? The noise had been deafening inside Nicole's head. Maybe the strength of Lila's thoughts had been heightened by her fear of being captured. Nicole would ask Maria if she would be a subject for further mind reading tests.

Maria did not have psychic powers, at least not yet. Maria was three years younger, and Nicole had not discovered her ability until she was 20. Maybe Maria would be like their mother, unable to read minds, or perhaps she might be a spotter, although those tended to be men.

Two years back, the sisters had decided to test their abilities, having heard the stories about the powerful women in their family. Maria went first, staring into Nicole's eyes. They both erupted into loud giggles. Maria tried again, and asked if Nicole was thinking of Cary Grant. Nicole had been thinking of an ice cream sundae. Then it was Nicole's turn, and for fun she wrapped her head in a turban. Maybe it worked, because she correctly read that Maria was thinking of a strict and difficult teacher at school, Sister Margaret Claire. They conducted further tests, concluding that Nicole did possess the gift.

Nicole was starting to doze by the time Maria finally appeared.

"Nic, are you asleep?"

"Almost. What took you so long?"

"I needed a good soak. What did you want to talk about?" Maria sat down on the bed opposite Nicole's and crossed her legs.

"This is something highly confidential. You must promise not to tell anyone, especially Mama and Papa."

"I swear."

"I'm going to hold you to that oath. I have been dating someone at work named Philip."

"Holy mackerel! Tell me about him."

"In a minute. I need a favor from you. I see Philip sometimes on my Thursday nights out with friends, and always on my breaks at work. He wants to take me out a week from tomorrow, so you will need to cover for me."

"What's wrong with him? I mean, why can't you tell Mama and Papa?"

"He isn't Italian."

"Oh, boy! That will go over well."

"Exactly. I would like to go out with him a week from tomorrow. Could you cover for me? We can leave together, and then you can do whatever you want. We will have to coordinate on the schedule."

"I will do it! Not just for you, but because it will help me too. Mama doesn't like my new friend Katie. I'm not sure why, but this way I can make plans with Katie that day.

"I really don't like sneaking around, but I feel I have no choice right now. Mama does have a lot of old world ways. I try to understand, but sometimes it's hard."

"Well, I'm in! So tell me about Philip! What's he like? If he's not Italian, what is he? Is he handsome? What does he do at the hotel?"

"Slow down, sis!"

Maria pushed herself up toward the pillow, and stretched out. "Okay, I'm relaxed. What's the story?"

Nicole started to fill Maria in on Philip, but she was careful not to let any details slip about the events surrounding the mind reading she had done for him. Maria was going along with Nicole's little romantic escapade, especially because she was getting something out of it herself. But Nicole wasn't sure whether her younger sister could be trusted to keep the mind reading incident away from their parents. A single juicy secret was enough for one night.

"He sounds dreamy," Maria said. "When can I meet

him?"

"If next Saturday works out, maybe we can plan something together after that."

"It will work out," Maria said. "I promise."

Nicole looked at her sister. She was sorely tempted to read Maria's mind, but that wouldn't be right. Nicole had her sister's promise, and that would be enough.

Chapter 16

The Uninvited

"Nobody can be as agreeable as an uninvited guest."
— Kin Hubbard

Exiting the streetcar at Babson Street, Lila walked to Regina Preston's place on Mildred Avenue in Mattapan, one of Boston's neighborhoods to the south. Mildred Avenue was an odd hybrid, with large businesses, such as Gentles Baking Company, on one side, and triple-deckers, tall homes with three flats stacked on top of each other, on the opposite side. Cousin Regina and her husband Earl lived on the second floor of one of the triple-deckers located directly across from Gentles.

Both Regina and Earl worked at the baking company, Regina in the office and Earl in maintenance. Lila had met Earl Preston only a few times, but she sensed he didn't like her much. Regina was sweetness personified, and Lila tried to emulate that when she was with family, but Earl probably sensed that something was off about his wife's cousin. Some people had that gift, although it was a curse as far as Lila was concerned.

Lila thought that Earl's attitude had infected his wife as well. While Regina still seemed like her sweet old self after she had married Earl, she was also more guarded with Lila. Maybe that was natural when a woman gained a new confidant through marriage, but something seemed off to Lila, and it was probably caused by Earl's mistrust.

Lila, known as Ruby back then, had sometimes seen cousin Regina at Nan's apartment, when Lila had visited from Tupelo during the summer. She didn't know much about Regina's family. The girls were not first cousins, she knew that much, but Lila hadn't been interested enough to sort out the details of the relationship. Even as a child, Lila only half-listened to things that didn't seem of use to her, and she couldn't imagine how Reggie's family history might be of importance.

Lila found the triple-decker, and climbed the short flight of stairs to the bottom porch. Entering through the front door, she walked up a longer flight of stairs toward Regina's apartment. She was about to knock on the door, when it opened, revealing Regina's smiling face.

"Welcome, Ruby. Please come in." Regina gave her cousin a hug after Lila had set her overnight bag on the hall table.

Putting on her "Ruby" face, Lila said, "Thanks, Reggie. You are so gracious, as always." Lila turned to Earl, who was reading a newspaper on the living room sofa. "Hello, Earl."

"Evening, Ruby."

"We'll be ready for supper soon," Regina said. "As I mentioned, potluck, just some leftover tuna casserole and warm bread. Let me show you to the spare bedroom, so you can get settled."

"I am so grateful, Regina. You are an angel." Lila glanced at Earl again, but he was hiding behind his newspaper.

Regina led the way to the spare bedroom. It was spare in more ways than one. The room had a twin-sized bed with a plain, beige bedspread, a small mahogany bureau, and a nightstand that did not match the bureau. Maybe they were saving the room for eventual children, Lila thought, although Regina wasn't getting any younger. Lila couldn't afford to be fussy, though, as Regina was providing a safe haven at a time when Lila had no other options. The convent decor would have to do.

At supper, Regina asked about Ruby's beau, Benny, as Lila had expected. Lila invented a quick story, explaining that Benny had cheated on her. Summoning her inner Sarah Bernhardt, Lila proclaimed, "I wasn't going to take that, cousin Regina. I just wasn't. I loved him, and he betrayed me." She figured such dramatic news would shut down the flow of questions. She was right.

Reggie said, "I don't blame you one bit, Ruby."

Even Earl said, "You did the right thing."

Satisfied that she hadn't aroused their suspicions in any way, Lila figured it would be best if she got out of the couple's way for the rest of the night. She complained of fatigue, reinforcing her cover story with the words, "the mice kept me up most of the night." Lila retired to her room with apologies. Regina and Earl looked relieved, so the evening had gone well overall.

When she got to the spare room, Lila opened her overnight bag. On top of the small pile of possessions resting inside, she found her tattered volume of *Sherlock Holmes Detective Stories*. Flipping to the table of contents, she located "A Scandal in Bohemia," satisfying herself that the story was still there, a scintilla of certainty at a time when everything had been upended. She jumped to page 132, and glanced at the story about a woman, Irene Adler, who gets the better of brilliant consulting detective Sherlock Holmes. Lila read the words, "In his eyes she eclipses and predominates the whole of her sex." She took a deep breath, feeling like there was more oxygen in the room after that.

Lila placed the book on the nightstand, and continued to unpack her few worldly goods. She pulled out her nightgown, a conservative blue number with a high collar trimmed in white lace, laying it out on the bed. *Thanks, Nan*, she thought. She looked at what was left in the bag, shaking her head. There really wasn't much to work with here, but it was all she had access to at the moment. Lila wondered if she could safely go back to Beacon Hill after laying low for a while. *I mean they can't watch that place forever, can they?* She had left a lot behind in those two apartments. Thinking of Beacon Hill made her remember the botched kidnapping and the mind reader. Lila had gotten a good look at her while the girl was standing on the street. The psychic's suit was definitely a uniform. She must work at the hotel. Was she in guest registration? Maybe she was an elevator operator.

I've got to make a new plan, thought Lila. *That girl is going to help me get those diamonds, and if not those, some other big score. I'll get in touch with Garrison tomorrow. He messed up her identification, so he owes me. I'm going to need some muscle to pull this off. Yes, I will start again tomorrow.*

Regina and Earl were staying home on Saturday, so Lila couldn't call Garrison from their apartment. Their phone was located in the front hallway, and she couldn't risk being overheard. She'd have to find a phone booth. Lila told them she was scheduled to work that day, and she left the apartment as though she was going to her job at the telephone company. It was too early to call Garrison, though, so she decided to explore the neighborhood and find a phone booth later. She saw there was a park in the opposite direction from the route she had taken when she arrived, so she headed that way. It looked like a nice place, with a playground and swings, although it wasn't very busy at that hour of the morning.

Lila crossed the street and headed up a hill. She had no idea where she was going, but roaming was appealing at the moment. It reminded her that she was still free. The street was called Fessenden, and it had a mix of housing types, single-family, triple-deckers, and brick apartment buildings. After walking past a synagogue, Lila found herself on Blue Hill Avenue, the street where the trolley ran. She spotted a drugstore on the corner of the street and decided to give it a try. As she entered the store, she could see they had a fountain with stools and a phone booth, which was tucked in the back corner. *Good*, she thought.

Lila picked up a copy of *Photoplay* at the small newsstand, and purchased the magazine. Then she ordered a Coca-Cola at the fountain. She browsed through photos of movie stars, while sipping her coke. She was waiting to phone Garrison, wanting to catch him late enough that he'd be alert, but early enough that he'd still be home after his Friday-night carousing. Timing was everything, Lila had learned.

As she sat at the fountain, Lila received some long looks from incoming customers, and she realized that people mustn't see many Negroes in this neighborhood. But it wasn't like where she came from in the south, where she would be forced to use a different entrance or sit in a separate section from White people. Here she could sit where she wanted to order a simple Coke, although some establishments might not be welcoming, especially in small towns. While some sidelong glances might have bothered Ruby Dubois, they meant nothing to Lila Laroche.

After about an hour, Lila arose from the fountain stool, and walked to the back of the drugstore, where the phone booth was located. She inserted a nickel into the phone, and dialed Garrison, finding him at home.

"Hello, this is Lila. I have some business to discuss."

"Hey, Lila. What's going on?"

"Well, Mr. Garrison, that was some bum information you sold me."

"Sorry, Lila. When I heard the Messina dame got snatched, I wondered whether I had fingered the wrong one. When people like me spot mind readers, our eyes get kind of fuzzy."

"Now you tell me. Well, what's done is done, but I figure you owe me."

"Yeah."

"Good, I'm glad we don't have to argue about this. I have a plan, but I'm going to need your help, gratis, of course.

"What's 'gratis'?"

"You're going to work for free, my dear, at least at the beginning. If things pan out, you'll get your part of the score."

"All right, lay it on me."

Lila laid out her big plan to Garrison. He wasn't much of a gang, but he was a start. She would be back on top in no time.

With her actual work completed early, Lila now had the rest of the day to fill. Regina and Earl would be expecting her home around suppertime, and since Lila held no real job at the telephone company, she needed something to do. While still positioned more or less comfortably on the tiny seat in the phone booth, Lila opened the classified telephone directory. Rifling through its pages, she searched for a few tidbits that might be helpful in planning her day. She found that there was a local branch of the Boston Public Library located on Hazelton Street and a movie theater called the Oriental on Blue Hill Avenue, both in Mattapan. Between these two places and anything else she found as she wandered, Lila thought she should be able to keep herself occupied for the day, without running into the Prestons in the process, she hoped.

Before leaving the drugstore, Lila stopped to ask for directions from the teenager behind the fountain. "Excuse me, young man. Can you direct me to Hazelton Street? I'm looking for the public library."

"Yeah, lady ... I mean, yes, ma'am. It's right near here." He ran out from around the fountain. "Come outside, and I'll show you."

She followed him out, and watched, as he pointed diagonally across Blue Hill Ave. "That's Hazelton right there, lady. You can't see the library from here, but it's not far from the corner."

It's right there? Lila thought. *That's unusually convenient.* "Thank you," she said. "You've been very helpful."

Lila crossed the avenue, and walked the short block to Hazelton Street, taking a right after passing a large apartment building. As the boy had promised, the library came into view immediately. It was a beautiful sight to behold, built in the

Classical Revival Style, with a rounded portico and a sloping green lawn in front. As Lila entered, she noticed the natural light afforded by the floor-to-ceiling windows, making the library a bright and welcoming place. She found the card catalog without asking for help, and looked up "Complete Sherlock Holmes," finding the call number and hoping the book was available. She was in luck! The two-volume collection was resting comfortably on a shelf in the "Adult" room. After grabbing the first volume, Lila flipped through its pages, finally landing on a short story called "The Final Problem." In this tale, another of her favorite stories, Sherlock Holmes and his nemesis, the criminal mastermind Professor Moriarty, both fall to their deaths after a struggle at Reichenbach Falls in Switzerland. Lila knew, of course, that Sir Arthur Conan Doyle had later resurrected Holmes for further adventures, but she never read those. She thought the series should have ended at the falls. Lila Laroche preferred to be the deceiver, not the deceived. She wasn't anyone's sucker. She began to reread "The Final Problem."

After spending her morning in the Victorian era with Sherlock Holmes, Lila came back to the present. She yawned, and then grabbed her pocketbook. Pulling out a slip of paper, she looked at the name and address she had written there. She walked to the librarian's desk, and in a low voice asked, "Can you tell me how to get to the Oriental Theater?"

"Of course, Miss. It's about a 15-minute walk from here. If walking is your preference, you would go down to the corner of Blue Hill Avenue, and take a right, following Blue Hill Avenue to Mattapan Square. The theater will be on the right side of the street. You can't miss it. If you would prefer to take the trolley, the stop is in front of the apartment building on the corner Hazelton Street and Blue Hill Avenue."

"Thank you," Lila said. "You've been most kind."

Lila made it to the trolley stop just in time to board the next streetcar. As she rode along, she noted that the avenue was a mixture of stores and residential properties until it reached Mattapan Square itself. The square was the commercial heart of the neighborhood, with businesses on both sides of the avenue, including the Woolworth's and Grant's chain stores, a bank, small restaurants, and, yes, The Oriental Theater.

Lila disembarked at the next stop, and headed toward the theater. She purchased a ticket for the matinee double feature, figuring the two movies should kill most of her afternoon. Stopping at the concession stand, she picked up a tub of popcorn and another Coke. Not much of a lunch, she thought, but it would fill her. As she explored the lobby, Lila examined the posters for the day's features. The show was an odd mix, opening with *Susanna Pass*, a western starring Roy Rogers and Dale Evans. Lila didn't much care for Westerns—not enough civilization for her. The second film, *Arson, Inc.,* looked to be more up her alley. It was a crime movie, and the poster advertised, "*Sensational Exposé* OF THE FIREBUG RACKET!" Lila wasn't attracted to fire, but she was always interested in criminal enterprises, even fictional ones.

When Lila entered the auditorium, she realized that the two movies wouldn't be the main entertainment of the day. The theater itself was the real star of the show. True to its name, The Oriental transported her to an ancient Chinese city, with high walls on both sides, and statues with eyes that glowed. There was so much to see, she didn't know where to look first. When she thought she'd seen everything, she rested her head on the back of her chair. Glancing upward, she saw a dark blue "sky" with "stars" that twinkled. When clouds started to float across the sky, Lila almost dropped her popcorn. Some apparatus high in the back was producing bursts of mist that resembled clouds. It was hard to believe that she was staring at a *ceiling*.

Viewing the auditorium's striking nighttime tableau reminded Lila of her desire to travel. She had never been out of the United States, and she wanted to see everything the world had to offer. She could do that someday, but travel required money. Luftman's diamonds would be her ticket to the world.

Chapter 17

The Best Prescription

"There is no such thing as a lovers' oath."

— Plato

Pat Messina had spent the weekend lounging and recuperating in her suite at the Hotel Manger. Her husband had never left her side. She slept, ate meals from room service, read magazines, listened to music on the radio, and slept some more. Teddy had wanted to call a doctor for her, but normalcy was what Pat craved most. "The best prescription," she had called it. She was grateful that he hadn't pressed the matter. The witch still appeared in her nightmares, and her shoulders ached from being tied up, but she wanted to maintain the sheltering cocoon with Teddy for as long as she needed it, no outsiders allowed. Room service had agreed to leave the cart with their meals outside the door.

At breakfast on Monday, Pat was lost in thought and found herself back in captivity at Lila's apartment. She said out loud, "That woman, Lila, was full of contradictions."

"Oh?" said Teddy.

Pat could see that Teddy had flinched when she'd

uttered those words, but he was trying to hide his discomfort, as though this subject was a typical one for their breakfast conversation. Poor Teddy. He had been through a lot himself. Pat pressed on nonetheless. "Yes, she kidnapped me, but she still seemed concerned about my comfort. I'm not sure what to make of that."

"I guess we should be grateful for whatever humanity remained in her."

"Yes. And grateful for Lieutenant Fitzgerald. We don't know that her humanity would have held out in the end."

"May I ask a question about what happened?"

"It's okay, honey. Go ahead."

"How did Fitzgerald find you?"

"He didn't say. I know the cab driver was downstairs in the police car. Maybe he got the information from him." They had been talking about the kidnapping for only a couple of minutes, and already she needed to deceive Teddy about something—the mind reader. Fitzgerald had said the unknown woman was the reason he had been able to locate Pat at Lila's.

"What's wrong, honey? We don't have to keep talking about this, if you don't want to," Teddy said.

"It's not that. There's something I'm not supposed to tell you. Fitzgerald asked me to keep it a secret, even from you. I'm not sure what to do."

"A secret? What could be so important that you can't tell your husband?"

"Fitzgerald received help from a woman."

"Why would that be a big deal?"

"That's where the secret comes in."

"Well, if you'd rather not ..." Teddy looked hurt.

"That's just it. I do want to tell you, but Fitzgerald said it could place the woman in jeopardy. He said she stuck out her neck to help me."

"We should thank her then."

"If the secret gets out, someone might grab her. That's the reason Lila kidnapped me. She thought I was someone else. The ransom demand was just a backup plan."

"Someone else?"

"Apparently I look like this woman."

"What? Oh my God, didn't you notice? The elevator girl looks like you."

"She does? I guess so, the hair at least."

"Why would someone kidnap the elevator operator?"

"Teddy, I trust you with my life, so I'm going to trust you with hers, but you must never tell another soul, and I'm going to ask you to promise, to swear on our marriage. She saved my life, so I must not jeopardize hers."

"I swear, honey. If she saved your life, I will not tell another soul." Teddy kissed her wedding ring.

"Thank you. Holding this back has made the situation even harder." Pat launched into the story, the mind reading, how she had played along, what Lila had wanted her to do, all the lurid details. She could see it was making Teddy nervous, and he started to pace the room. Pat was sorry she was agitating her husband, but, at the same time, getting this out was making her feel better. Well, not completely better. She wasn't keeping her word to Fitzgerald about not telling Teddy.

When she finished, Teddy ran over to her. "I'm so sorry. That must have been terrifying." Pat could see that he was trying to hold back tears.

"We have both been through a lot," Pat said, starting to cry too. She stood up and they held each other. "We will be okay. It will take time, but I know we will be okay."

"I'm sure we will," said Teddy. "We need to say thank you to that girl, Nicole. She probably saved your life."

"I don't know if we should. I promised Fitzgerald I wouldn't tell you."

"But we must thank her. Don't you think she would want to know that we appreciate what she did?"

"I guess so. He just made such a big thing out of it."

"We will assure her that we'll keep it confidential. I'll call Altman and ask him to send her up, saying we want to thank her before we check out."

"Won't that make him suspicious?"

"I don't think so. She helped Fitzgerald with the stenography. And now I see there was more to that than meets the eye. But that will be our excuse."

"Yes, let's do that. I really would like to thank her."

Teddy headed to the phone and dialed the assistant manager. "Hello, Mr. Altman. This is Teddy Messina. I'd like to talk to you about one of your employees, Nicole Rossi."

Chapter 18

A Perfect Day

"And we find at the end of a perfect day,
The soul of a friend we've made."

— Carrie Jacobs-Bond

Nicole reported for work on Monday as usual. She was looking forward to seeing Philip on her break so she could give him the good news about their Saturday plans. Maria was willing to cover for her, so Nicole and Philip could spend the day together like a real couple. What would they do? With all the strategizing over the plan with Maria, they hadn't even discussed how they would spend their afternoon together.

After several rides up and down in her elevator, Nicole was waiting in the lobby for more passengers, when a hotel messenger arrived with a slip of paper for her.

"Hey, Nicole, you must really rate. You've got a message from Altman."

"Thanks, Rawhide." Nicole had no idea why people called him that, and she really didn't want to find out. Hesitating to open the note, she thought, *Now what?* The message was in Mr. Altman's bold handwriting, with letters almost an inch high, and it told her to visit the Messina suite as soon as possible, giving no reason. Nicole had once been so bored at her job, but lately she had found herself praying for a simple, dull day.

She rode straight to the 17th floor, hoping to get it over with, whatever "it" was. Locking down the elevator, Nicole gazed at her reflection in the brass control panel to make sure she was presentable. She would do. She approached the door to Messina's suite with a feeling of dread, but finally worked up the courage to knock.

Teddy answered, saying, "Hello, Nicole. I'm glad you're here. Please come in."

"Thank you, Mr. Messina."

"Please call me, Teddy."

"It may take me a while to get used to it, but I'll try to remember ... Teddy." As Nicole entered the suite, she saw Pat sitting at a room-service table. "Oh, I'm sorry, I didn't mean to disturb your breakfast. My supervisor sent me a note saying I should come up here right away."

"Don't be concerned," said Pat. "I was just finishing up. Please sit down and make yourself comfortable."

Nicole sat down on what by now had become her usual chair, still wondering why she was there.

Teddy cleared his throat, and began. "Nicole, we want to thank you. We know you are the woman who helped Lieutenant Fitzgerald find Pat."

131

Nicole felt her stomach lurch.

"We want you to know that Fitzgerald never told Pat your identity, but Pat already knew that Lila had been out to kidnap a mind reader. Once we noted your resemblance to Pat, not to mention your association with Fitzgerald, we put two and two together, figuring the mind reader must be you. We want to assure you, though, that your secret is safe with us. We will be checking out tomorrow, and we felt we couldn't leave without saying thank you from the bottom of our hearts. You probably saved Pat's life."

Pat arose from her chair and approached Nicole. "Is it all right if I give you a hug?"

Tears started to well up in Nicole's eyes. "Yes ... that will be ... fine," she said.

The two women embraced, and Pat said, "If you ever need anything ... anything at all, please call on us. I'm going to give you our personal number." Pat passed her card to Nicole.

"Thank you," Nicole said, wiping away some tears.

Pat took a few steps toward an end table and picked up a flat, pink box. Pulling out a lace-trimmed handkerchief, she handed it to Nicole. "Here you go," Pat said. "In fact, please accept the entire set. It's my favorite design. Don't worry, I have more."

Nicole had never seen such an elegant hankie in her life. "These are beautiful," she said.

"A small token," Pat said. "Teddy has something else to tell you that I think you'll like."

Nicole turned toward Teddy, unsure of what to expect.

"I have also mentioned your help to Mr. Altman," he began. "Not your secret ability, of course, but your help with the stenography. I also mentioned that you have conducted yourself in a professional manner. I hope that will lead to a promotion for you, if you're interested in one."

"I am, um ... Teddy. Thank you so much." Mixed emotions were becoming a regular part of Nicole's life since she did the favor for Philip. On the one hand, two more people knew her secret. Could they be trusted? On the other hand, she had a recommendation from Teddy Messina and the personal card of his wife. Once again, she wasn't sure what lesson she was supposed to be taking from all this.

Nicole was ready to burst at the seams by the time she met Philip for break. She started talking before she even hit the seat.

"So much is happening! I don't know where to begin."

"Slow down, honey. What's going on?"

Nicole started with the news from Teddy and Pat. She lowered her voice as she described their acknowledgment of her mind reading ability, but she couldn't restrain her excitement when she mentioned Teddy's recommendation to Mr. Altman.

"Wow!" said Philip. "Life can be strange. This whole thing started because I wanted a recommendation from Teddy, and you got one instead."

In her exuberance, Nicole hadn't thought of that. "I hope you're not upset, honey."

"I'm a little jealous, but I'll get over it. I'm happy for you."

Philip wasn't a very good actor, and she could see he was disappointed. Nicole wanted to tell him what had happened at Lila's place, but thought she should hold that for now, and spring her other good news, the news about them. "I think this will cheer you up. Maria has agreed to cover for us! She is going out with her friend Katie, while I see you. What shall we do on Saturday?"

"Hey, that is great news! I'll let you choose the plan. Anything but a movie, after what happened last time."

"Hmm ... nothing fancy ... I think I'd like to go to Bailey's for an ice cream sundae and then take a walk in the Public Garden. We are starting to see some fall color. Is that too simple?"

"I like that plan, as long as the weather is good," Philip said.

"When shall we meet and where?"

"Let's meet in front of the Manger, and then we can take the train from North Station. How does 2 PM sound?

"It sounds perfect. I will tell Maria. We'll leave the house together at 1:45 PM. I'll be praying for sun!"

"Or at least no rain. It's a date!"

Nicole felt ecstatic. Now she just needed to come up

with a story for her parents about what she and Maria were going to do.

Philip interrupted her thoughts. "You never told me what happened with Fitzgerald at Lila's."

"I'll tell you later. Let's just enjoy this."

At work on Tuesday morning, Nicole was still consumed with thoughts about her impending date with Philip. She offered passengers on her elevator distracted "hellos," as they entered the car. Nicole continued to puzzle over what she should wear for her Saturday afternoon date. Philip usually saw Nicole in her uniform, so she wanted to dazzle him with something special. On her salary, though, there wasn't much that was dazzling in her closet. She also didn't want to raise her parents' suspicions, since she was supposed to be having just an afternoon out with her sister. After some consideration, she decided to go with her teal blue dress. It was an everyday number with a wide collar and matching belt, and she frequently received compliments on it. She'd have to decide on Saturday whether to wear her trench coat or white sweater over the dress, depending on what the weather looked like.

A little after 9:30 AM, the hotel messenger arrived with a note for Nicole, as she waited in her elevator.

"Hey, Nicole, you've got another message from Altman. What makes you so special?"

If he only knew, she thought. "You're supposed to deliver

the messages, Rawhide, not ask questions about them."

"Sorry, *boss!*"

"You're forgiven, Rawhide."

He waited while Nicole opened the note, and she shooed him away.

What could Altman possibly want now, she wondered. She read the short message. "Please visit the Messinas in their suite as soon as possible." Nicole couldn't imagine why they wanted to see her again, but she would be more than happy to visit Teddy and Pat now. The worst was over, after all. She shot like a rocket up to the 17th floor.

Pat answered the door. "Please come in, Nicole. We are checking out today, and wanted to say goodbye to you."

Nicole thought they had done that yesterday, but who wouldn't want to spend more time in a beautiful hotel suite with these wonderful people.

She walked into the suite, and saw that Teddy was wearing a broad smile. "Hi, Nicole!"

"Good morning, Teddy!"

Pat looked pleased with herself. "Thanks for coming, Nicole. We have a little surprise for you. Please close your eyes."

"Surprise?" Nicole was startled. Surprises weren't her favorite thing lately.

"C'mon, Nicole," Pat said, giggling.

Nicole did as she was asked, and Pat placed a small package in her hands. "Okay, Nicole, you can open your eyes now."

Nicole complied, and saw a box, expertly wrapped in shiny silver paper with a white bow on top. "What's this?" She asked.

"It's for you. Open it," Pat said. "It's a small token of our appreciation."

"You didn't have to do that. You already gave me those beautiful handkerchiefs."

"Those were something I already had. This is especially for you."

Nicole hesitated, but finally started to open the gift. She removed the silver paper carefully, as though it were the gift itself, and placed it on a side table. When she saw what was underneath, she gasped. The writing on the box said "E.B. Horn." Nicole knew that Horn's was a famous jewelry store in Boston, but she had never gathered up the courage to go inside. When she opened the velvet box, she found a stunning pearl bracelet inside.

"Oh, my gosh! This is so lovely! Pearl is my birthstone!"

Pat and Teddy looked at each other, smiling. "We know. Teddy asked Mr. Altman when your birthday was. He said we wanted to add you to our list for birthday cards."

"But this is much too generous ..."

"You saved my life. Measured against that, it is nothing."

Nicole was so excited that she rushed forward to hug Pat, and didn't stop there, embracing Teddy as well. She suddenly felt embarrassed at her boldness, but the three of them were so happy it didn't matter.

Teddy said, "Let's see how it looks on your wrist."

Nicole placed the box on the table, and rolled up the right sleeve of her blouse and suit jacket.

Pat offered to help, removing the bracelet from the satin-lined box. After fastening the pearls to Nicole's wrist, she said, "Perfect!"

Teddy agreed. "Those really suit you."

"Thank you so much," Nicole said. "I've never owned anything so beautiful in my entire life." She turned her wrist this way and that, admiring the luster of *her* white pearls. *What's Philip going to think*, she wondered. *Oh ... Philip! What time is it?* She glanced at the beat-up watch on her other wrist, which looked even more shabby to her now. "I hate to run off," Nicole said, "but I'm supposed to meet my friend downstairs soon. I'm so grateful for this exquisite gift, and I will always cherish it."

"We are so happy you like it," said Pat. "And please remember to use that phone number I gave you, if you ever need anything. We will always be there for you, if we can."

"Thank you," Nicole said.

Pat kissed Nicole goodbye, and Teddy gave her a hug.

Nicole was practically dizzy by the time she reached the elevator. This was all too much, and she was running late for Philip on top of it. She figured if she took the elevator straight down, and headed immediately to the break room, she would be only a few minutes late. Philip would understand, especially when he heard the reason.

Nicole arrived in the break room frazzled, but happy. When Philip started to ask where she had been, she slowly pushed back her sleeve to reveal the bracelet.

"What the ... ?"

"It's from Pat and Teddy," she whispered. "A thank you gift."

"Are those *real?*"

"I couldn't exactly ask, but I'm pretty sure they are. They came from E.B. Horn!" She slid the velvet box out of her pocket to show him.

"Holy mackerel!"

"I know! I've never had anything like this in my life! Of course, I have a problem now. How am I going to explain these to my parents? I really want to wear them."

"Yeah, you can't exactly tell them you've received pearls for saving Pat Messina's life," he whispered.

"Right. And even celebrities don't give away pearls for elevator rides."

"Hmm ... what about the hotel's lost and found raffle? You could say you won them. Sometimes there's some pretty nice stuff in lost and found, and there's actually another raffle coming up soon."

"That's a great idea! Wait, now you're coming up with lies for me too. I thought Fitzgerald was bad enough." Nicole shook her head.

"I guess you can just hide them in your purse."

"So my choices once again are lying to my parents or deceiving them."

"Sorry," Philip said. He looked at her wrist. "They sure are beautiful. You deserve to wear them."

"Let me think about it," she said. In the meantime, she flashed the pearls in front of Philip.

He took her hand, solemnly bowing his head toward her. "Your Ladyship," he said.

Nicole burst out laughing, and Philip followed, drawing the attention of everyone in the break room. She quickly lowered her sleeve, and they suppressed further giggles, but Philip gave her one of his winks. She did love that boy.

When Saturday rolled around, Nicole and Maria left the house together as planned. Nicole figured that sticking close to the truth was always best, so when she told her parents about the afternoon's agenda, she simply substituted Maria for Philip in the plan she had already made. That way she would have details of both Bailey's and the Public Garden, if needed. Maria would have to let Nicole do the talking, if they were questioned. Nicole wondered whether she was getting a little too good at producing an easy lie, but she brushed that idea aside in favor of concentrating on a pleasurable afternoon.

The sisters departed at 1:45 PM. It was a crisp, sunny day, so the weather had cooperated. Nicole was wearing her white sweater over the teal dress, and she had hidden the pearl bracelet in her pocketbook. She hadn't decided whether to tell her parents the "lost and found raffle" story about the gift, but she certainly wanted to wear it today on her date with Philip.

They met Maria's friend, Katie, at the corner of Salem and Prince streets. Nicole could see that Katie was fully committed to the bobby-soxer style. Maria's friend sported white socks, loafers, rolled-up blue jeans, and a boy's jacket. Mama would definitely not have approved. The girls were a bit mysterious about their plans, but Nicole had decided not to press them. Maria had reassured her that everything was on the up-and-up, and Nicole assumed that her sister wouldn't want to jeopardize the plan, in case they wanted to do it again.

Nicole was right on time to meet Philip at the Manger. Philip lived with his parents and sisters in the West End of Boston, on Poplar Street, so the Manger was a convenient, central place for the couple to rendezvous. There was no phone at Nicole's house, and Philip wouldn't have been able to call her without raising suspicion anyway, so she was to check for a message at the front desk if he was more than 10 minutes late.

As she waited for Philip, Nicole suddenly felt strange. It was almost as though she could sense the presence of Lila Laroche in the vicinity. The area around the hotel was always crowded, with both Boston Garden and North Station nearby, but she did her best to check the faces of people walking by. Nicole had received an image of Lila from reading Pat's mind, but she couldn't be sure how accurate it was. Lila's face flashed only briefly, alternating with the more lingering image of the witch's mask.

Nicole's eyes were drawn to a man, who was neatly dressed, although his suit was out of style. He wore a dapper hat, also old-fashioned, and he had a nicely trimmed mustache. *Well, that can't be Lila,* she thought. Nicole was confused and a little afraid, but Philip seemed to appear out of nowhere in front of her.

"Everything okay, honey? You look nervous."

Nicole did not want to spoil their first Saturday date, especially over something that might be her imagination, so she said nothing. "Everything is fine now that you're here," she said.

"Good. Let's get this date started." Philip took her hand, and they headed to North Station.

Nicole kept her eyes on the crowd. The feeling that Lila was nearby had disappeared, as had the dapper gentlemen. *Enough with this foolishness,* she thought. *I'm not going to let ANYTHING ruin this date.* She squeezed Philip's hand as they boarded the train to Winter Street. Time for their date.

Nicole and Philip entered Bailey's from West Street. They walked through a long, low hallway, which suddenly opened into a large room with a high ceiling. The effect was as though one had discovered a secret place in the heart of downtown Boston. Small tables with ice-cream-parlor chairs filled the space.

Philip had been to Bailey's before, but it was a new experience for Nicole. They found a table, and ordered traditional ice cream sundaes. While Nicole was taking it all in, Philip took her hand. "Hey, where's your bracelet?"

"Oh, it's still in my pocketbook. Would you put it on for me?" She removed her sweater, placing it on the back of her chair, and then took the bracelet from her purse, passing it to Philip.

He fastened the pearls to her wrist, saying, "Hey, they look even more beautiful with that dress."

She beamed. "Thank you, honey."

He blew her a kiss.

Nicole was loving the date so far, but she was shocked when their order arrived. The sundaes were served in small, metal dishes, and the hot fudge poured over the sides onto matching plates below. Part of the fun was eating the sundae from the bottom plate. Philip dipped his index finger into the hot fudge below his dish, planning to smear it on Nicole's nose, but she was ready with spoon in hand, threatening to catapult ice cream at his new shirt. It was a draw, and they giggled through the whole experience.

Their next stop was the Public Garden, located next to Boston Common on Charles Street. They headed right away to the Foot Bridge, where they stood in the center, looking out over the Lagoon. Philip slipped his arm around Nicole's waist, and she returned the favor, placing her arm around him.

Although the garden's Swan Boats stopped running in September every year, Nicole imagined that they were still gliding majestically through the water. As a boat moved under the bridge in her daydream, she could see herself sitting with Philip on one of its benches.

Afterwards, they strolled around the water's edge, enjoying the graceful weeping willows and the fall colors, which were starting to appear on the elms and other trees. They found a bench, and Philip put his arm around Nicole, who rested her head on his shoulder. They didn't talk a lot, sensing that words might get in the way of the special gift they had been given. It had turned into the perfect day.

Chapter 19

A Man of Few Words

"All the world's a stage ...

And one man in his time plays many parts ..."

— William Shakespeare

L ila Laroche returned home on Saturday afternoon, well before Reggie was due to arrive. Laroche used the key her cousin had given her, but went through the back door of the apartment. No sense raising suspicion, given the way she was dressed. Earl was working, and Regina was volunteering at something or other, so Lila had plenty of time to change out of her men's clothing. She called her disguise "Gerard," and "Gerard St. Cloud," his full name, had been useful to her in certain circumstances, as when he dealt with Jacoby, her building manager, or when Gerard had followed the mind reader near North Station.

The mind reader had met a young man, and the two of them had disappeared into the station, so "Gerard" had thought it best not to follow them. The psychic's friend looked to be a sturdy fellow, and it was best not to draw attention to Gerard at this point anyway. It had been a positive result nonetheless, as the visit had established the psychic's continued connection to the Manger. Staking out the hotel again would be the best option for finding out more about the girl, and doing it in the guise of Gerard would be the safest way for Lila to operate.

Lila's abrupt departure from Beacon Hill over a week ago had forced her to leave a lot of Gerard's clothing in her apartment. She had resorted to purchasing some used men's clothes from Morgan Memorial for today's outing, although the new Gerard was more old-fashioned than his predecessor, but no less a gentleman.

Nan had once told Lila a story about enslaved women in the South, who had posed as men to escape captivity. Lila had pricked up her ears then. She did listen when Nan started to say something useful, and Lila had remembered the story when a disguise later became necessary. Gerard St. Cloud was born.

Lila suddenly heard the sound of a key sliding into the front-door lock. *Oh no!* There was no time to change clothes. She would have to talk her way out of this. Laroche could see cousin Regina coming through the door. "Reggie, it's me, Ruby. Don't be afraid! I'm not an intruder."

"Ruby? You almost scared me to death! Why are you dressed like that?" Regina's right hand was on her heart.

"I'm sorry, cousin. I auditioned today for a part in a play at The Footlight Club in Jamaica Plain. The character has to disguise herself as a man, so I was showing off my abilities in that area. I didn't mean to scare you. I just got home myself, and haven't had time to change."

"You always were creative, Ruby. Did you get the part?"

"I don't know yet."

"If you get it, let us know. I'd like to take Earl to see your play. We could use more culture in our lives."

"I would be honored to have you attend." Lila made a gentlemanly bow.

Clapping her hands, Regina said, "Bravo! That's wonderful, Ruby. I bet you will get the part. Earl will be shocked to see you this way!" She laughed. "Speaking of Earl, I need to ask you something. You've been staying with us for over a week. We want to help you out, of course, but we are wondering what's happening at your apartment. It seems as though the mice situation should have been resolved by now."

Lila looked out the window at the Gentles Baking Company sign, as though she might find inspiration there for her next excuse. "I'm so sorry, Regina. I really don't want to impose. The mice apparently caused some damage, so a little carpentry work is also needed. I'm hoping to be back in my apartment later next week. In the meantime, I will be getting paid on Monday, so I will give you some money for room and board then."

"That's not necessary, Ruby. You are family."

"I insist, Regina. It's the least I can do. You hadn't planned on another mouth to feed."

"Okay, thank you, Ruby."

Lila noted that Regina looked relieved. That would

probably get Earl off of her cousin's back for a little while, but Lila's days on Mildred Avenue were numbered.

It was clear that Lila had to get her hands on some cash soon. She had almost depleted the funds hidden in her overnight case. Laroche needed to make a contribution to placate Regina and Earl, but she also had to arrange some new accommodations. It had been over a week since she had narrowly escaped capture at the hands of that plainclothes detective, and she wondered whether police would still be watching her Beacon Hill place. She had a stash hidden in Nan's apartment, and that would come in handy right now. She decided that it might be safe for Gerard to visit Phillips Street. If anything looked amiss, he would get right out of there.

Lila and Gerard had kept to themselves, so she wasn't too worried about running into neighbors, but Jacoby would be a problem. He was always home. She knew, however, that he did go out on Monday mornings for shopping and errands, so that would be her best time to visit Beacon Hill. She had a narrow window of time in which to accomplish her mission, but it should be enough.

Lila left Regina's apartment as Ruby on Monday morning, apparently heading to work, but then she doubled back after Regina and Earl had left. She changed into her Gerard disguise, and departed again.

As she rode the streetcar to Egleston Station, Lila

wondered what challenges she would encounter at Nan's. Police would be the big issue, of course, but if the cops had staked out the apartment, they had probably given up by now, considering her long gone. More likely, they had told Jacoby to let them know if Gerard or Lila reappeared. Another question was whether the lock had been replaced on the door. It probably had, but Gerard was a good lock picker, so that should be no impediment. The plan would work.

Lila made her connection at Egleston, and took the train to Summer Street downtown. No one was paying her much mind, so her disguise wasn't ringing any alarm bells. She had perfected her Gerard makeup, posture, and attitude through years of practice. Lila walked up Winter Street, crossing Boston Common, and was alert as she approached Phillips Street on Beacon Hill. She used her best Gerard walk, a little class and a little swagger, as she navigated the neighborhood. She kept her eyes moving, but didn't see anything suspicious.

At last she reached Nan's apartment, and felt confident enough to enter. As expected, Gerard needed to pick the lock, but his skills were equal to the task. Lila knew right where she needed to go once inside, so it would be a precision operation. She located the carpet sweeper in the kitchen closet, and found the cash right where she had left it, in the sweeper's internal compartment. She rifled through the bills, and the money was all there. Next she moved to Nan's bedroom closet, and picked up a small suitcase. Lila had a few of her own clothing items here, so she packed them in the case. She was in and out of the apartment in less than 10 minutes.

Lila thought she was out of the woods, but when she turned onto Anderson Street, she ran smack into her building manager, Mr. Jacoby.

"Mr. St. Cloud! Good day! I haven't seen you in a while. I'd like to talk to you for a minute."

"I'm in a rush, Mr. Jacoby. Can it wait?" Lila's natural speaking voice was low to start with, and she added a rasp, which Gerard claimed was due to a war wound. He wore a cravat to cover the scar on his neck. Gerard's injury made him a man of few words.

"I will be brief, Mr. St. Cloud. The police are looking for your sister. They say she kidnapped someone! You should get in touch with a Lieutenant Fitzgerald at the Joy Street Police Station right away."

"Oh, dear. My sister was always the bad apple in our bunch. I will check in with the police right away," Gerard rasped. He tipped his hat to Jacoby, and was on his way. Gerard walked at a steady clip until he was out of Jacoby's sight. Then Lila picked up the pace, as she was sure Jacoby would call the cops immediately.

Lila beat a hasty retreat to Mattapan, where she transformed herself back into Ruby Dubois. She later left the apartment so she could arrive home from "work" at the usual time. Well, it had been work in a way. She gave Regina $5 toward room and board, which seemed to satisfy her. Things were falling into place for Lila's new start.

Chapter 20

Who Is Gerard St. Cloud?

"Every man at the bottom of his heart

believes that he is a born detective."

— John Buchan

Lieutenant Jack Fitzgerald sat at his desk in the Joy Street Police Station. He reached for his neglected coffee, but the mug felt cold, so he gave it a pass, his thoughts returning to Lila Laroche. She was still at large, and he felt confident that his early assessment had been correct—Laroche had left the area. His men had kept an eye on her Phillips Street addresses for almost a week, but she hadn't been spotted. Otherwise there was little to go on with this woman. He was still looking, of course, but "Lila Laroche," "Lila St. Cloud," and "Gerard St. Cloud" were all phantoms. The name on Lila's second apartment, the one where she had held Pat Messina captive, was Mrs. Phoebe Dubois, and Fitzgerald had traced Dubois to the Crestwood Convalescent Home in Roxbury, where she was a resident. He had tried to question Mrs. Dubois, but her answers had not been coherent. The old woman's rent was up-to-date on Phillips Street, so Laroche must have been paying that. Fitzgerald was looking into any relatives Phoebe Dubois might have, particularly a Lila Dubois, but if Lila was from the South, as Pat Messina had reported, the quest would be difficult. When Jack had searched both of Lila's apartments, he had found no photos or records. Lila had been careful.

Jack snapped out of his contemplations, when the phone rang. "Fitzgerald," he said.

"Good morning, Lieutenant Fitzgerald. This is Mr. Jacoby at Phillips Street. I'm calling to let you know that I ran into Gerard St. Cloud today on Anderson Street."

"You saw him? Did you speak with him?"

"Yes, I told him that the police were looking for his sister and that he should check in with you."

"When was this?"

"About 20 minutes ago."

"Well, if he was walking, he should have reached the station by now."

"He said he would call on you right away, but he had indicated that he was in a rush when I stopped him. I should also mention that he was carrying a suitcase."

Damn, thought Jack. "I don't think we'll find him now, but I'll send some men out to scour the area. What was he wearing?"

"He was well dressed, as usual, but his suit was a bit out of style, gray with a vest. He always wears a cravat to cover his neck, and he wore a hat."

"What size was the suitcase?"

"It was small. It looked more like a woman's suitcase."

"Hmm ... Tell me, is there a resemblance between St. Cloud and his sister?"

"I should say so. They both have very prominent dimples when they smile."

"Good. I'll add all of this to his description. I'm going to come over and take a look around the two apartments again. Will you be home for the next hour?"

"Yes, I will be here for the rest of the day."

"Okay, I'll be there soon. I will need the keys to both apartments."

"I'll have them ready."

"See you then. Thanks."

Fitzgerald glanced around Jacoby's apartment. It was extraordinarily neat, with not one thing out of place. The furniture wasn't new, but all the pieces matched and were highly polished. Jack figured that Jacoby had a lot of time on his hands. As an overworked police detective, Fitzgerald was too busy for such a neat apartment.

"Mr. Jacoby, tell me more about your encounter with Gerard St. Cloud."

"There isn't much to tell. I spoke with him just briefly. Mr. St. Cloud doesn't say much. As I told you last week, he has a war wound, an injury to his throat, which makes his voice sound very raw. I imagine it is uncomfortable for him to talk."

"Does anything else come to mind about him or the meeting?"

"Oh, he did describe Miss St. Cloud as the bad apple in their bunch."

"This is helpful, Mr. Jacoby. Thank you for calling us. Now I'd like to take another look at both apartments." Fitzgerald had learned that Jacoby managed the apartments in several of the row houses on this side of the street. "I'll return the keys when I leave."

"I hope you find something useful to your inquiry," Jacoby said. "I still find this all so hard to believe."

"I see some unbelievable things in my line of work," Jack said. "I'll be back soon."

Fitzgerald walked down the stairs to St. Cloud's apartment on the first floor. Examining the new lock on the door, he found no signs of tampering. He let himself in using the labeled key from Jacoby, and scanned the living room. Everything appeared to be in order. Next he went to check the secret door inside the bedroom closet. Although his men had bolted the door from the closet side, so no one could use it to access the apartment from the basement, he double-checked the security measures. Lila Laroche seemed to be such a magician that he needed to make sure the bolts were still in place. No one had gotten through the secret door.

As he walked a couple of doors down the street to the row house that contained the Dubois apartment, Fitzgerald wondered about the relationship between Gerard St. Cloud and Lila. Given the resemblance noted by Jacoby, they were most likely a real brother and sister, but were they also partners in crime? Or was Gerard just the brother who bailed his sister out of jams?

Fitzgerald arrived at the door of Phoebe's apartment. The new lock there had some scratches along the keyhole, indicating that the lock had most likely been picked. He tried turning the doorknob, and the door opened easily. Without a key, St. Cloud would have been unable to lock the door upon leaving. This apartment had clearly been his target. Since Jacoby had mentioned a suitcase, Fitzgerald checked all the closets. The presence of some empty hangers in one of them led Jack to believe that St. Cloud had taken some clothing. It was starting to look like Gerard might be helping out Lila Laroche. That meant that she was probably in the area. But where?

Fitzgerald glanced at his watch. *Still plenty of time*, he thought. His son was playing a Maple tree in his school's Fall pageant, and Jack had promised to be there. The job had caused him to miss a lot of family appointments when he was married, and he had vowed to do better. He needed to be there by 3 PM, so he would leave no later than two o'clock to allow for traffic. There was enough time to head back to the station and consider all the things he had learned today about Lila and her brother. Then he would forget them both for a while and drive to Cambridge, where he would watch his son be the best damn Maple tree that Notre Dame de Pitie grammar school had ever seen.

Chapter 21

A Break in the Case

"No memory is ever alone; it's at the end
of a trail of memories, a dozen trails that
each have their own associations."

— Louis L'Amour

The Saturday date with Philip had been a dream, and Nicole was still thinking about it at work on Thursday. She hoped for another chance when Philip next had a Saturday off. Maria was already bugging her about doing it again, because she wanted to see her friend Katie.

Their secret plan had gone like clockwork. Maria and Nicole had met at 5:30 PM after their dates, and the sisters had returned home together. Mama had asked about Bailey's, and Nicole had described the messy ice cream sundaes. Mama wasn't a big fan of mess, so she didn't need further details. Papa was listening to opera in the parlor, so the girls were in the clear. More Saturday dates were in the offing.

Nicole knew that she would have to tell her parents about Philip soon. She just wished that Fitzgerald would find Lila, and then Nicole could feel that her mind-reading secret had been contained. How much longer should she wait? She'd give it until Thanksgiving, and then assume Lila was gone. Nicole would go ahead and spill the beans to her parents at that point. Such an important conversation would take some planning.

Unfortunately there would be no Thursday-night date after she finished work today. Philip was scheduled for the evening shift and none of her other work friends were available. Nicole had made plans to shop with Maria at Filene's Basement instead. She had told Mama they would be home for supper.

Nicole punched out and headed to meet Maria in front of the hotel. She hoped her sister would be on time. As she stood waiting, Nicole got that weird feeling again, the one where she sensed the presence of Lila Laroche. Nicole's eyes scanned the area, and she noticed the same dapper gentleman she had seen the last time she had experienced that strange sensation. He was even wearing the same clothes. What was going on? The man was standing across the street, and a car with its motor running was resting at a nearby curb. She focused on the dapper man, trying to read his mind. As impossible as it seemed, the man was Lila Laroche! Lila and the driver were planning to follow Nicole and grab her when the coast was clear. Nicole could see a picture of the spotter, the one who looked like Bogart, in Lila's mind, and thought he might be the car's driver. And there was that image of diamonds again.

Nicole stood as close to the lobby doors as she could. She wished Maria would hurry up and get there. When she finally saw her sister, Nicole ran forward and grabbed her hand. "Maria, thank God. Let's go inside!"

"What's happening? I thought we were going shopping."

"I will explain in a minute. We've got to get inside!"

"You're scaring me!"

Nicole pulled her sister into the lobby of the Manger. Philip was standing near the front desk and ran over. "What's wrong? You look scared to death."

Nicole whispered something in Philip's ear, and he ran outside.

"Sis, please tell me what's going on!"

"In a minute. Let's wait for Philip to come back."

"That's him? Your Philip?"

"Yes."

Philip came running back. "I didn't see them. Are you sure?"

"Positive." Nicole whispered something else to Philip. He dashed over to a phone booth.

"Maria, I'm going to tell you something. Once again I am swearing you to secrecy. Let's go up to the lounge. We'll be able to talk more privately there. Philip has gone to call the police."

"The police?"

"Follow me," Nicole said.

The lounge was empty, except for one man, who was reading a magazine in a soft chair. Nicole pointed to the other side of the room, and Maria followed. Once settled on a sofa with wide stripes, Nicole started to speak. "I can't tell you the whole story right now, so I'm going to be direct. I'm sorry I have to be so blunt. I used my power as a favor to Philip, and a spotter saw me. The spotter mistook Patricia Messina for me, and Pat was kidnapped instead."

Maria gasped.

Nicole continued. "The woman who kidnapped Mrs. Messina, Lila Laroche, escaped, and now I think she is after me."

Philip interrupted them at that point. "Fitzgerald is on his way." He sat down on the sofa, and put his arm around Nicole. "Are you okay?"

"I am feeling better now, honey. Let me introduce my sister, Maria. Sis, this is my friend ... boyfriend, Philip Kozak."

Philip arose and shook Maria's hand. "Nice to meet you, Maria. Thanks for helping us out on Saturday."

Maria looked stunned. Nicole's sister continued to be unusually quiet. Finally Maria said, "Hi, Philip."

"I hope you ladies are all right." Philip sat down and squeezed Nicole's shoulder again. "I thought Lila was long gone."

"So did Fitzgerald," Nicole said.

As if on cue, Fitzgerald appeared near the lounge stairs. Nicole wasn't sure if Maria was ready to absorb anything else, especially her older sister's connection to a police lieutenant, but she would have to grow up a little today. "Hi, Jack, this is my sister Maria."

"Nice to meet you, Maria. Are you ladies all right? Hey, Kozak."

Everyone exchanged greetings, and then Fitzgerald took charge. "Maria, I have to talk to your sister in private. Why don't you grab a magazine. Kozak, I assume you need to get back to work."

"Yeah, Lieutenant." Philip turned to Nicole and took her hand. "I'll see you later, honey."

As Philip walked away, Fitzgerald said, "thanks for phoning me, Kozak."

Good, he's warming up to Philip, Nicole thought. She and Jack moved over to the corner desk, which had by now become "their spot," while Maria got hold of a magazine. Nicole began to tell Jack her story about the dapper man who had revealed himself to be Lila Laroche through a mind link.

"Well, I'll be!" Jack said. "This explains so much! I never considered that a woman would disguise herself as a man ... well, maybe in a Shakespeare play, but not in the real world. I've got to hand it to her. That Lila is an original. So Gerard St. Cloud is Lila Laroche!"

"She is daring, that's for sure!"

"And tenacious. And maybe not as smart as she thinks. She should have left town on the first train. Instead she's still thinking about diamonds. By the way, did you get the license plate of the car or can you see it now in your mind?"

Nicole tried to call up the scene from memory. "Sorry, Jack, I was concentrating on reading his ... I mean ... her mind."

"It's okay. This is a good break in the case. We don't have to keep searching our files for Lila's brother Gerard any more. He doesn't exist."

"I know that's good news, but I can't help thinking that on any other day, I would have been walking straight home. They might have snatched me!"

"I don't even want to think about that. I'm glad you're all right." Fitzgerald gave Nicole's hand a squeeze. "I think the danger is gone for the moment, but I'm going to drive you two home. How much does your sister know?"

"I told her the basics. She got very quiet. Usually you can't shut her up. I guess I'll have to make up a story for my parents about what happened, a stomach ache or something. I'm getting tired of all these lies."

"Do you think your sister will go along with the story?"

"Given some recent experience, I would say yes."

Jack raised an eyebrow, but kept his thoughts to himself. "Okay, let me drive you ladies home. I'm going to pick you up for work tomorrow too. What time do you leave?"

"7:30. You can't come to the door."

"I figured that out for myself. I'm a detective, remember? I'll wait down the block."

"Okay, thanks."

Nicole went to get Maria, and then Jack drove the sisters to their home in the North End. Nicole went over the cover story with Maria. It was low on details, just that Nicole had experienced a sudden stomach ache, and thought it best to go home.

"Can you do this?" Nicole asked.

Maria nodded.

"Try to be your usual talkative self when we go in," Nicole said, "or they'll know something's wrong."

"I'm going to complain of a stomach ache too. Maybe they'll think we're getting the flu."

"Well, I don't want to worry them."

"I think the real reason would worry them more."

"Good point."

Nicole's little sister was coming back to herself.

The sisters had toast and tea for supper in their room. A light supper was a small price to pay for having deceived their parents about the real events of the afternoon. Nicole hadn't intended to involve Maria in another deception, and she certainly hadn't planned on exposing her to the crime element in her recent life, but today's developments had been out of her control. Her sister seemed to be sleeping soundly now, so that was a good sign.

Nicole herself was having trouble finding rest. Her mind was crowded with thoughts. Would Lila come after her again?

Was her family safe? When would this all be over? She took some deep breaths, and started to relax. Had she missed anything? Jack had wanted the license plate of the car. She called up the memory again, but still couldn't see the license plate. Was there anything else she could give him? Nicole tried to search Lila's thoughts, as though she was standing directly across the street from her ... make that, Gerard. Yes, the diamonds were there. Lila really wanted those jewels. *Huh.* Suddenly Nicole was seeing a long building. The sign said "Gentles Baking Company." It was as though she was seeing it through Lila's eyes. What could that mean? You wouldn't keep diamonds at a baking company, would you? Well, she would tell Jack when he picked her up tomorrow. If Lila was thinking about it, it was probably important.

Chapter 22

Diamonds Aren't Forever

"No pressure, no diamonds."

— Thomas Carlyle

Everything was in place. Lila Laroche's contact at the jewelry store knew the rescheduled delivery day for the diamonds at last, but he didn't know the time or any other details. The plan was firmly lodged in the head of his boss, Mr. Luftman, who wasn't opening that door to anyone. But Lila had or would soon have a key to unlock that door, the mind reader. Granted, things hadn't gone well the first time, when Lila's minions had kidnapped the wrong woman, and Luftman had gotten roughed on top of that, but Lila was doing things herself this time. She knew who the mind reader was now, or at least what she looked like and where she worked. Lila just needed to grab her with Garrison's help. There would be no mistakes this time.

Dressed as dear brother Gerard, Lila positioned herself across the street from the Hotel Manger on Thursday afternoon. Garrison waited nearby in a banged up 1941 Ford, and he had muddied the license plate to make identification difficult. When the girl left work for the day, Gerard would follow her on foot, while Garrison stayed close in his car. They would wait until the psychic hit a secluded spot, snatch her, and then take her for a ride to Luftman's store. Lila's contact would make sure the back door was unlocked. Luftman remained in the store every day for an hour or so after closing, counting up receipts, so he would be alone. And if they never found the girl in the clear while she was walking, they would follow her home and learn her address. If this plan didn't work, the next one would. The mind reader would help them to make a big score one way or the other.

The girl departed the hotel a few minutes after 4 PM, just as Lila had hoped. *She is pretty, I'll say that*, thought Lila. *And she does look like Patricia Messina. If Garrison's vision was diminished by his ability, I can see why he made that mistake. Oh, no. Why is she stopping?*

The mind reader appeared to be looking for someone. Then she spotted Lila and stared for a minute, returning to her search after the pause. Lila hoped this snafu wasn't going to ruin her second chance at the diamonds. If the girl was waiting for a friend, they couldn't grab both of them. Two against two was not a desirable ratio for a kidnapping.

The girl kept scanning the area. Finally she seemed to spot the person she was waiting for. It was a younger girl, with dark red hair, her sister maybe, and the mind reader ran toward her, taking her companion's hand and leading her back into the hotel.

What the hell? Lila got into the passenger side of Garrison's car, and started banging her fist on the dashboard. "I can't believe this! It doesn't look like she's going home right now. On top of that, she's got a friend. I think today's plan is dead in the water. The diamonds are due tomorrow, so that's that." Lila switched from banging her hand to stamping her feet like a child. She finally took a deep breath to calm herself. Lack of control was the enemy. "I need to come up with a new scheme. This girl will be the death of me."

"Maybe you should forget about her, Lila."

"I don't believe in failure, especially at the hands of a little nobody. I'll come up with another score. Then we'll pick her up some other day."

"If you say so."

"I do say so. You owe me, remember?"

"Yeah, I remember."

"Good. Take me back to your place. I've got to change." Lila couldn't arrive at Regina's in men's clothing again. There would be too many questions to answer about the nonexistent play, so she had to take off her makeup and change clothes. She rode with Garrison to his hole in the wall, which made Regina's apartment look like the Taj Mahal. Lila transformed herself into Ruby again, scrubbing her face clean, and putting on a plain white blouse with a navy blue skirt.

Garrison laughed when he saw the change. "You look better as Gerard."

"It's just another part I'm playing," Lila said. "Are you

167

going to drive me home?"

"Uh, it's a lot of gas to Mattapan and back to the West End."

"Don't do it for Ruby. Do it for Lila." She was aware that Garrison didn't know what to make of her. Her main power over people was that off-kilter quality she possessed, with its hint of danger. Lila used that to her advantage. She wasn't sure anymore whether that was yet another part she was playing or the real her.

"All right, let's go," Garrison said.

"That's more like it. When we hit it big, remind me that I owe you for gas money."

Garrison dropped Lila off at the corner of Babson Street, and she walked to Regina's apartment from there. She didn't arrive home much later than usual, so Regina didn't ask where she had been. Unfortunately her cousin did have another question for her.

"I'm sorry to bring this up again," said Regina. "We were very grateful for your contribution for room and board, but you also mentioned that you would be back in your apartment later this week. Tomorrow is Friday. What are your plans?"

Damn! Earl is behind this, Lila thought. She tried to retain sweet Ruby's countenance so she could avoid shooting daggers at Earl. Lila needed to think fast. She would have to escalate her lies. It was a risk, to be sure, but the mice scenario was as dead as the mice themselves should be by now. "I am so ashamed, Regina," she began. "I have been lying to you right from the start. I was fired from my job. I told you my boss hated me." Lila pulled a tissue from her sleeve. "I couldn't pay my rent and had to leave my apartment. Some of my belongings are stashed with various friends. I was just so embarrassed for our family." Lila held her breath.

"Oh, honey, you should have told us right away. People get fired. It isn't a crime."

"Thank you, dear Regina. You have a good heart." Lila grasped her cousin's hand. It looked like Regina had fallen for it, but then Lila glanced at Earl. She wasn't as sure he was convinced.

"So, where have you been going every day, Ruby?" Earl asked.

"I've been looking for work, Earl. Sometimes I visited friends. I'm sorry I deceived you. Now that you know, I guess there is no harm in asking. Are there any jobs available at Gentles?"

"We will definitely inquire for you, Ruby. Don't you worry," Regina said.

Lila had bought herself more time, but she would have to get out of the Prestons' apartment soon. Knowing her cousin Regina, she'd have a job interview lined up for Ruby on Monday. This could get awkward fast. She'd take some of her stash from Nan's and go looking for an apartment. Then she'd tell Regina she had found a job in town. A few more days, and Lila's exile in Mattapan would be over.

Chapter 23

A Drive to Mattapan

"Wherever you go, go with all your heart."

— Confucius

Nicole left for work on Friday morning as usual. She walked up the street, and found Jack waiting in his car, as he had promised. She knocked on the window, and he waved her inside.

"Good morning," said Jack.

"Hi!" said Nicole.

Jack pressed the starter on his Chrysler Imperial, and pulled the car away from the curb. "So how was your night?" he asked.

"I've had better," Nicole said. "I was restless—too many thoughts rushing through my mind."

"I know the feeling. How's your sister?"

"Maria seemed to sleep soundly. She's always been a good sleeper. She was quiet at breakfast, but didn't give anything away about Lila and her intentions." Nicole shuddered, thinking about how close she had come to being kidnapped.

"I'm glad she's playing along. Your sister seems like a nice kid."

"She is, just a little over-enthusiastic sometimes. She was definitely not herself yesterday." It was just a short ride from the North End to the Manger, so Nicole wanted to get to her Lila news right away. "Jack, I remembered something last night that I had picked up from Lila's thoughts. It came to me after I relaxed a bit. There was an image in her mind of a place called Gentles Baking Company. I don't see how that could be connected to diamonds, but I thought I should tell you. Have you ever heard of it?"

"I've seen their bread and cakes in some stores around town, but I don't know where they're located. It might not be related to the diamonds, but maybe it is a clue to where Lila is hiding out. I'll get hold of a telephone directory when we reach the hotel, and see if it's listed there. Boy, would I like this to be the big break in the case."

"It might be. I feel this is important, Jack. That's not coming from mind reading, at least, I don't think it is. It's just a regular old hunch."

"Fingers crossed," Jack said, acting out the words with his right hand.

When they arrived at the hotel, Nicole went to punch in, while Jack searched for a phone book. He caught up with her at the elevator bank. "Let's talk for a minute." They walked around the corner and sat on the low bench in the lobby. "Gentles Baking Company is located in Mattapan. This isn't a lot to go on. Can you tell me anything else?"

"It's like she's looking at the sign from the outside, not inside the building, in a lobby or something."

"That's good. Maybe she is hiding out somewhere near the company's headquarters. I'm planning to take a look around there, but it would be nice if I could narrow my search. There might be three-deckers or apartment buildings there. I could use your help, if you're willing. Maybe you can figure out the vantage point, or something like that. What do you think?"

Nicole sighed. "I think I'm tired of this, but, at this point, if it will help find Lila, I'll do it. I've never been to Mattapan. When do you want to go?"

"I'll get you out of work early today, say 3 PM. I'll tell your boss I want to take you out as a thank you for all your help."

Nicole frowned.

"I'm going to do that, by the way. I promise! But not today. Today we're going to Mattapan."

Philip will not be pleased, Nicole thought, *but at least it will be a change of scene.* She was almost looking forward to it.

After a ho-hum morning in the elevator, Nicole met Philip in the break room.

"Hey, honey, how are you this morning? That was a weird situation yesterday."

"I know. It never seems to stop." She filled him in on

her new revelation about Lila, and told him about the trip to Mattapan.

"I don't like this, Nic," Philip said. "It could be dangerous. Fitzgerald shouldn't be taking you out with him on an investigation."

"I will just be there to help identify the house, or the 'vantage point,' as he called it. He will bring me home right afterwards. Then he'll go back with his men to knock on doors later. I will be safe. Please don't worry."

"But I do worry."

"I'm sorry, but this could turn out to be the big break in the case. If we can get Lila behind bars, then we will be safe."

"All right, but please don't take any chances."

"I promise I won't take any chances," she said, forming her right hand into the three-fingered Boy Scouts' sign.

Philip laughed. "You're the cutest Boy Scout I've ever seen, but I mean it. Be careful. I'll be holding Fitzgerald personally responsible. I don't know about that guy. He takes advantage of your abilities, and it's clear he doesn't like *me* at all."

"He thinks you're a pretty boy, and pretty boys get away with too much. He's probably just jealous."

"Well, I am a pretty boy," Philip said, winking at Nicole.

"Yes, and we all know you know it," she said, rolling her eyes.

"Me?" Philip pretended to be offended, placing his hand over his heart, but Nicole knew otherwise. "And I do get away with some things, especially at home," he said, "but in case the big detective hasn't noticed, I am a bell boy. It's not like I've been given the keys to the city."

"He's warming to you, honey, I can tell. Just give him a little time. But here's something I know you will like better. I've decided to tell my parents about you, whatever happens with this Lila mess. It might not be today or tomorrow. I need to think about the best time and the best way, but it will be soon. I don't want to wait any longer. That favor I did for you has taken control of our lives, and I'm tired of it. I'm going to take charge of my own life again."

Philip smiled. "Well, that *is* good news. I like that way of thinking."

"I thought you would like it." She reached for his hand, on top of the table this time.

Jack picked up Nicole at 3 PM, as planned. Although he usually wasn't prompt when he was coming from the station, Jack was on time today. Nicole had emphasized that she didn't want to get home late. It was an old story by now, and she was tired of that one too.

Despite the reason for the trip, Nicole was looking forward to the ride. Her parents didn't have a car, so she seldom ventured out of the North and West Ends or downtown. She had once taken a vacation to Waterville, Maine with a friend, but that was the extent of her worldliness. She asked Jack to talk about points of interest on the way, and she drank in every drop as they cruised along. They passed Fenway Park, home of the Boston Red Sox, with its high wall, and a place called Emmanuel College. When Jack told her it was a Catholic college for women, Nicole's eyes grew wide.

At last they left the city buildings behind, and entered an area which had trees on one side and residential homes on the other. They drove by a picturesque body of water, and Jack told her it was called Jamaica Pond. The trees around the pond were changing into their fall colors, and Nicole thought it was a beautiful sight. Jack seemed to know every twist and turn of the streets in Boston, and Nicole marveled at his expertise.

They reached a street called Blue Hill Avenue, and Jack turned on to it. He told Nicole that they weren't far from their destination now. A streetcar ran along this stretch, and Nicole noticed businesses here, as well as three-decker homes and apartment buildings. The avenue was wide and seemed to go on forever, a far cry from the congested streets of her North End. They took a left turn onto a street called Fessenden, and a quick right and then left onto Mildred Avenue. She spotted a playground with a stone field house, before the road made a sharp right angle, after which Nicole could see triple-decker houses on one side of the street and several businesses on the other. Jack pulled over in front of Gentles Baking Company.

Gentles occupied several buildings, which took up the width of about six housing lots. The sign was the one Nicole had seen in Lila's mind, so they were in the right place. "This is it, Jack," she said. They exited the car to look around.

"Let's cross the street," Jack said, "and see if we can figure out where she was watching from. I was hoping there would be single-family homes, but at least they're not apartment buildings."

They crossed the street, and Nicole paced back and forth, twisting her head this way and that. "I think it is one of these two houses," she said, gesturing behind her, "but the angle is wrong. It's like she was looking down from somewhere." They both looked up. "It could be from a window or a porch," Nicole said.

"That's good," Jack said. "Well, that will give us four apartments to check out, the second and third floors of each house. That's narrowed it down a lot. Plus, you have confirmed we are in the right place. Good work!"

Nicole felt a surge of pride. "Thanks, Jack!"

"I promised to bring you home early, so let's get going."

Nicole turned around to look at the houses once again. She felt another surge, but it wasn't one of pride this time. It was something else, a sensation that was becoming all too familiar. "Wait, Jack," she said. "We shouldn't leave just yet."

Chapter 24

Stay or Go?

"Know when to fold. Pay attention

to the signs. They're there."

— Molly Bloom

Regina and Earl Preston were at work. At least Lila didn't have to pretend she was going to her job anymore. She was planning to relax for the few days she probably had left on Mildred Avenue. It would depend on whether Reggie lined up an interview for her. Lila supposed she could go on a job interview. It could be a bit of fun. *How do you do, sir? Yes, my life's ambition has always been to clean toilets.*

Taking a sip from her coffee mug, Lila opened the newspaper to the classified ads section. Locating the apartment listings, she began to scan them. Lila wasn't going to get far on her stash from Nan's apartment. She had really been hoping to get her hands on those diamonds. *That damn mind reader!* Were there any other cards she had left to play? How long would Reggie and Earl allow her to stay? What if she actually got a job? She had held only one honest job in her whole life, and she didn't like to think about it. Nan had told her she needed to earn her keep when Lila had visited during the summer before her 17th birthday. Nan had lined up a job for Lila, well, Ruby, as a maid at a rooming house in the South End. Lila quickly learned that cleaning up after yourself, and maybe your family, is tolerable, but cleaning up after others is disgusting. It put her off honest work forever. In that light, her life of crime was really Nan's fault. No, she wasn't interested in a job per se, but a job *interview* could give her the chance to case the baking company. They must have some funds in a safe or a lockbox somewhere. That might lead to a different sort of job opportunity, but maybe it wasn't a good idea to pull something this close to home. Something to think about.

Holding her coffee mug, Lila stood up and looked out the window. There was that Gentles Baking Company sign again. What signal was it sending? "Stay" or "go"?

Her musings were interrupted by voices on the street, and Lila looked down to find the source. She gasped. It was that detective! And the mind reader! What were they doing here in Mattapan? Lila thought for a minute. There was only one conclusion she could draw. The woman had been able to read her mind from a distance! *How could I have been so stupid? It wasn't Benny or Jacoby who fingered me. It was that girl!*

The question of whether to stay or go had been decided for Lila. She had to go, and go *now*. Lila wasn't sure what the mind reader's range was, but she needed to get as far away from that girl as she could. At least she had treated herself to some of her own clothes today, the ones she had picked up from Nan's apartment. Her pants would be easier for running than one of Ruby's ridiculous dresses. She dashed to the bedroom, and opened the closet. There were no hidden panels here, and no secret tunnels below. She felt a sense of loss, but there was no time for emotion now. She was here for a jacket and her stash. She grabbed both, stuffing the cash into her pants pocket. Lila ran out the back door and down the stairs.

Where should she go? The cop was on the street, so she would keep to the backyards. That should give her a good head start. She had been a sprinter in her day, so she should be out of there in no time. Maybe she should run up Fessenden Street, and then hide in one of the apartment building alleys until the trolley came. That should do the trick. She had her stash. It would be okay.

Chapter 25

Moving Pictures

"The art of motion pictures is pictorial and
language comes a distant second."

— Jean-Jacques Annaud

Nicole pointed at the gray triple-decker house with white trim. "Jack, Lila knows we are here! She's running out the back door of this house right now!"

"You stay put, Nicole! Get in the car and lock the doors." Jack ran to the back of the house.

Nicole did what she was told. She turned to look out the window, but instead saw a moving picture that was beginning to play inside her head. Nicole realized she was viewing the world not through her own eyes, but through Lila's. Laroche could see Jack coming around the side of the house, and she was starting to run. Nicole didn't know how she could help Jack, but she felt pulled to the backyard. She got out of the car, and rushed down the driveway beside the house.

It was hard for Nicole to see, as she had two sets of images in her head, one provided by her own eyes and one coming from Lila. The pictures kept alternating, and she was confused. She started to wobble a bit, and moved toward the side of the house to steady herself. Lila was running and had come to a fence. She was going to climb it. Would Jack be able to catch her? Leaning on the house for support, Nicole rounded the corner, and found the backyard. She didn't know why, but she felt compelled to yell, "Lila, stop!" Laroche stopped in mid-step. Jack ran over to Lila and placed handcuffs on her. Through Lila's eyes Nicole looked down at the handcuffs on her wrists. Then the image cut away, and Nicole's vision returned to normal.

As Jack walked Lila out of the yard, he whispered to Nicole, "What happened?"

Nicole said, "I don't know!" She noticed that Lila's face looked blank, like she was in some kind of trance. From everything she had heard about Lila Laroche, Nicole would have expected her to put up a fight, but Lila was as gentle as a lamb. Nicole turned to follow Jack out of the yard.

As Nicole stepped onto the sidewalk, she almost ran into a woman, who was about to enter the backyard. The lady said, "Hello, Nicole. My name is Regina Preston."

"How do you know my name?"

"Please don't be alarmed. I'm like you, a mind reader. My cousin is the woman you know as Lila. To me she is Ruby Dubois. Why don't we sit down for a minute?"

Jack rushed over, interrupting their conversation. "I've called for a squad car. Lila is handcuffed in the back of my Chrysler. Who is this?"

"This is Regina Preston," Nicole said. "She is Lila's ... uh, cousin."

"What? No offense, ma'am, but something crazy is going on here."

"I think it's okay, Jack." Nicole turned away from him and toward Mrs. Preston, saying, "This is Lieutenant Jack Fitzgerald of the Boston police."

"How do you do, Lieutenant Fitzgerald?"

"I'm not exactly sure at the moment," Jack said. He extended his hand to Mrs. Preston. "Sorry, ma'am. Has Lila Laroche been staying with you?"

"Yes, she has, although I know her as my cousin Ruby Dubois. I wasn't aware that she had broken any law until you arrived."

"I don't understand," Jack said. "You just got here. How do you know she broke a law?"

"I have the same power as this girl. I know you are aware of her ability. I received the information from her."

Jack and Nicole looked at each other.

Regina said, "I'd like to talk to Nicole, if I may. I want to explain what happened just now with Lila. Nicole needs to understand. We'll sit up on the porch, where you can watch us. Normally I would prefer to do this in private, but since you already know about her powers, you may join us too. It's up to the two of you."

"I'll wait down here with the prisoner," Jack said. He looked at Nicole.

"It's all right, Jack," Nicole said. "I'm not afraid."

Once the two women had settled on the porch swing, Regina began to explain what had happened. "Your thoughts came to me at work, Nicole. I was across the street at the Baking Company."

"My thoughts came to you?" Nicole had heard only two sentences, but she was already astonished. She knew she still had a lot to learn about mind readers, and here was her first direct contact with someone like herself. Her only source of information prior to this had been her mother, who had passed on stories from relatives long gone before Nicole had even been born. She had so many questions to ask this woman, but sat back, allowing Regina to take the lead.

"We worked together, Nicole, you and I, to stop my cousin. I tapped into your power to gain control of Ruby."

"Gain control of Ruby? How is that possible?"

"Let me explain. I have the power to control some minds, but I don't use it often. Wielding it comes with consequences, but I made an exception in this case, once I had learned from you what Ruby had done. Eventually you may gain that power as well."

Nicole was having a hard time believing Regina's words. Mind control? It seemed like something from a B movie. While her mother had mentioned that particular ability before, Nicole hadn't been sure whether to believe her. And yet, what other explanation was there here? Lila had stopped in her tracks. "Why did you need to tap into me?"

"I have never been able to read Ruby. It happens occasionally. Some people are easy for you to read, some hard. It's almost like frequencies. You are tuned into certain ones, and I may be tuned into others. For some reason, you are very tuned into Ruby. I was practically blind to her. On the other hand, you were like an open book to me, at least in your moment of distress. It was like your channel was open, and your thoughts floated over to me in the bakery. So when I realized what was happening, I used you as a conduit to control Ruby's mind. It didn't make me happy to do it, but it had become clear that she had caused a lot of trouble, so I didn't see an alternative. I hope you think I made the right decision. I'm sure it must seem strange to you that I used you like that."

"Yes, it is very strange, but I think you made the right decision. We haven't had much peace with Lila ... um, Ruby on the loose." Nicole saw the squad car pull up, and Jack went over to talk to the officers.

"I'm glad you agree with my decision. I sense that you're alone with your power. Is that true?"

"Yes, unless my younger sister gets it."

"Please feel free to call me, if you need someone to talk to. It can be hard to adjust, especially if there's no one to guide you."

"Thanks. I'd like that."

Just then a man came running along the sidewalk and up the stairs. "Reggie, what's going on? Are you okay?"

"I'm fine, Earl. Unfortunately, Ruby is in some trouble

with the law."

"I'm not surprised," Earl said.

"Nicole, my husband was always suspicious of Ruby, but he is suspicious of everyone, so I shrugged it off."

"Now you know better," said Earl.

"Oh, hush!" Regina said. "Where are my manners? Nicole, I think you have figured out by now that this stern-looking fellow is my husband, Earl. Honey, this is Nicole. She's a new friend. I will explain the details of what happened later."

Earl shook Nicole's hand.

Jack reached the porch at that point, having just sent Lila off in the squad car. He still looked out of sorts, but he extended his hand to Earl. "I am Lieutenant Jack Fitzgerald of the Boston police. I assume you are Mr. Preston?"

"Right."

"I understand that you didn't know you were harboring a fugitive. I will need to talk to you both about that later."

"We are happy to cooperate. What is the charge against Ruby?" Earl asked.

"Kidnapping, among others."

"Whew! Ruby didn't fool around."

"She surely did not. I need to get this young woman home, but I would like to call on you tomorrow. Will you be at home?"

"We plan to be home all day," said Regina.

"Very good. Expect me around mid-morning."

Nicole and Regina arose from the porch swing at the

same time. Regina started to shake her hand, but Nicole gave her a hug. "Thank you for everything you did today," Nicole said. "I'm hoping my life can return to normal now."

"I hope so too, but you must understand that normal will be different for you going forward."

That wasn't exactly what Nicole wanted to hear, but she knew she would need to accept the new reality. Not only were her powers increasing, but she had become aware of another with even greater abilities than she had. She could worry about those issues later, though. For now Lila was off the street, and that was a huge burden off of her shoulders. She and her family were safe! Next she needed to tell her parents about Philip. She would focus her attention on that and forget about Lila Laroche, Ruby Dubois, or whatever her real name was.

Everyone said goodbye, and Nicole turned to Jack. "I'll explain everything in the car," she said.

"I will be all ears," he said. "This sounds like a doozy."

"You have no idea," said Nicole.

Chapter 26

A Tough Spot

"In tough times, we all hope for knights in shining armor,

or the cavalry, to show up and effect change."

— Dean Devlin

T he sidewalks glowed in the setting sun, and Lila felt at peace. She was riding in the back seat of a car, and the gentle rhythm of the wheels as they rolled along the asphalt was soothing. Whose car was this? She looked around, but had no sense of recognition. She tried to move her hands, but they resisted her. Then she sensed the cold steel on her wrists. She was handcuffed! *This is a police car! WHY?*

The last thing Lila remembered was seeing that detective in Regina's backyard. Had she passed out? Had the mind reader mesmerized her? She had heard stories of mesmerists, people who had the ability to control minds, but she had thought they were folktales. Imagine what she could do with that ability! She would be out of this mess in no time. Could the girl actually have the power? That would make her the most special of the special.

Lila tried to piece together what had occurred. She

vaguely remembered wanting to climb a fence. Someone yelled "stop!" Probably the cop. Why had she stopped? Was there something wrong with her? She couldn't check her head easily while wearing the handcuffs, but she felt no pain in her head or anywhere on her body, for that matter.

Had she seen Regina walking toward her on the sidewalk? Maybe not. Everything was so jumbled. Would Regina look for her or report her missing? *She will probably just say "good riddance,"* Lila thought. Ruby had definitely overstayed her welcome with the Prestons. *Regina is so dull, happy in her tiny apartment with Earl. Good riddance to them too*, she decided.

Two uniformed officers were sitting in the front seat of the cruiser. "Excuse me, officers, I believe I have some sort of head injury," she said. "I have no memory of how I got here."

"The lieutenant didn't say anything about an injury, but we can get you checked out at the station," said the one riding in the passenger seat.

"Thank you, officer. That's very kind. I know my memory is foggy, but I don't believe I have committed any crime. It must be some kind of misunderstanding."

"The lieutenant said the charge was kidnapping, among others. Sounds serious."

"Kidnapping? That doesn't sound like me."

"You can tell your story to the judge."

"If I can remember it," she said, thinking she might be able to use the memory angle to her advantage. She might as well start laying the foundation now.

Lila Laroche had been in tougher spots before. Well, not really. The charge was kidnapping this time. But up until this point she had always landed on her feet. She would prevail again. She could really use Gerard's assistance right now. The real Gerard, Gerard Dubois, her long-lost brother, make that half-brother. He had been her teacher in her late teens, introducing her to fine books and social graces, as well as con jobs and heists. It had been a wonderful whirlwind, but it ended when Gerard thought she was becoming too reckless. I guess she had proven him right by risking the kidnapping. She needed to get in touch with Gerard. He wouldn't leave her to rot in jail for years on a kidnapping charge, would he? She would have to do the thing she dreaded most, calling her father's first wife. If anyone knew where Gerard was, it would be his mother, Everline Dubois. Everline was not Ruby's biggest fan, and the feeling was mutual. Lila knew that tracking Gerard down would take time, but he was her only hope. He had the resources and the skills to spring her, but would he have the nerve? Until she located Gerard, Lila would be forced to enjoy the hospitality of some prison warden or other in Massachusetts.

Captivity! Her worst nightmare. Her dreams of traveling the world dashed. Lila would gladly accept the confinement of Benny's Shangri-La at this point. He had envisioned her as a queen there, never aging, seeing her enemies dead. Now if she were lucky, she would be the queen of cell block C. How had it come to this? It was that mind reader. It always came back to *the girl*. Lila would get her revenge some day, somehow, but for the moment, she was out of options.

Chapter 27

A Flicker of Doubt

"Doubt is not a pleasant condition,

but certainty is absurd."

— Voltaire

"We did it, kid! Well, you did it. I just brought the handcuffs." Jack reached for Nicole's arm and shook it with his right hand, while keeping his left hand on the steering wheel of his Chrysler.

"To be honest, Jack, Regina did it."

"You'll have to explain that to me, but I would point out that if you hadn't known Lila was fleeing, Regina's help probably wouldn't have mattered."

"Good point. Plus, Regina wouldn't have been able to reach Lila's mind without me. She said I was her ... 'conduit.'"

"That's the part I'm not clear on. Please lay that out for me."

Nicole explained how Regina was mind-blind to Lila. Since she couldn't reach Lila herself, Regina had used Nicole's open link to Lila, sending the order for Lila to stop running.

Nicole described the "frequencies" comparison as best she could. "Can you imagine, Jack? Mind control! It must be very rare. Regina also mentioned that there are consequences when she uses it, but she didn't say what they are."

Jack didn't want to admit it to Nicole, but he was uncomfortable with the idea of mind control. While it had helped them catch Lila, it was disturbing to think that there were people out there who could control one's thoughts and actions. It gave him the willies. Would Nicole gain this ability eventually? Her powers already seemed to be increasing. What would it mean for her future? She was a wonderful young woman, and he wanted her to have a good life. Jack would keep an eye on her. He wasn't sure how he could help her, but he would be there if she needed him.

Jack guided the car toward downtown, reversing the route he had taken to Mattapan. The setting sun caught the leaves of the trees around Jamaica Pond, creating a ribbon of golden light.

Nicole pointed at the trees, saying, "Look, Jack! It's so beautiful."

When Jack glanced at her hand, he caught sight of a pearl bracelet on her wrist. "New bracelet?" he asked. "That seems expensive for a gift from Kozak."

"Oh, it's from Pat and Teddy Messina. It was a thank-you present."

"What were they thanking you for? Surely not the stenography."

"For saving Pat's life. They figured out that I was the mind reader. Don't worry, Jack. They told me you didn't reveal my secret."

"What? She promised not to tell her husband. I told Mrs. Messina not to say *anything* about the mind-reading angle of this case."

"They were so appreciative, Jack, and felt they needed to do *something*. Pat also gave me her card in case I ever need anything. They are really lovely people."

"I hope so. Celebrities adore publicity, and you are a *good* story."

"I think it will be fine, Jack. They promised not to tell a soul, and I believe them."

Jack began to worry about Nicole's future again, as the tall buildings of the city loomed on the horizon. Could the Messinas be trusted? He hoped so. He had to agree with Nicole that they seemed like sincere people, and they knew what was at stake after Pat's own kidnapping. Well, Lila Laroche was in custody now, so there was no point in worrying about things that hadn't happened yet. He decided to change the subject. "Nicole, any big plans for the weekend?"

"The biggest, Jack. I'm planning to tell my parents about Philip."

"They don't know already? I thought you two were an item."

"We are, but my parents are old-fashioned and don't want me to date boys who aren't Italian. I've been sneaking around. Jack, I've been keeping so many secrets!"

"You poor kid. I didn't realize. Maybe they will take it better than you think."

"I hope so!"

"I'm not sure how I can help, but if there is anything I can do, please let me know."

"I thought you didn't like Philip."

"I may have misjudged him. He's okay for a pretty boy."

"You must have been a pretty boy, Jack."

"Thanks ... I think." Jack supposed he should take that as a compliment. He didn't hear many flattering words about his looks these days. Yes, she had seen something in him. He'd leave it at that.

Fitzgerald drove back to Mattapan on Saturday morning. He didn't want to bother the Prestons too early, but he hoped to have time to throw a football around with Jimmy in the afternoon. He arrived a little after 10 AM, knocking on the Prestons' door.

Mrs. Preston answered. "Good morning, Lieutenant. Please come in."

"Thank you, Mrs. Preston. I hope not to take up too much of your time today."

"Would you like a cup of coffee?"

"That would be nice, thanks."

Mrs. Preston poured Jack a cup of coffee from the

percolator, and set the cup in front of him on her enamel kitchen table. "Please help yourself to some cream and sugar. The coffee might be a little strong by now."

"I like my coffee strong, thanks." Jack opened his notebook. "So, Mrs. Preston, you are a blood relation of the woman you call Ruby?"

"Yes, we know her as Ruby Dubois."

Jack wrote that down. "What is the familial relationship?"

"Ruby is my second cousin. Her father and my mother were first cousins."

This is helpful already, Jack thought. "Do you know where Lila, I mean, Ruby, grew up?"

"Ruby grew up in Tupelo, Mississippi. I was born here, and I saw Ruby during summer vacations, when she visited her grandmother, my great aunt Phoebe, on Beacon Hill. Ruby and I are close in age, so Aunt Phoebe encouraged our friendship."

Jack was scribbling like mad, when Mr. Preston entered the room. Jack stood up, and they shook hands. "Good morning, Mr. Preston."

"Good morning, Lieutenant," Mr. Preston said, sitting down at the table next to his wife.

Jack said, "Ruby fled her two apartments on Beacon Hill. How ..."

"Two apartments? Beacon Hill? We thought she had a place in the South End," Regina said. "She told us she had vacated Aunt Phoebe's apartment after settling my aunt's affairs there."

"How did she come to stay with you two?"

"She called me one day from Egleston Station, and said she was having a mice problem at her apartment. She said she couldn't bear to spend one more night there, so we agreed to let her stay with us until the exterminator came. More lies followed."

"I always told Regina that Ruby couldn't be trusted," said Earl. "I was right."

"Lieutenant, I've been hearing 'I told you so' since yesterday!"

Fitzgerald smirked, then carried on. "Did she entertain any friends while she was here?"

"No one. She pretended to go to work, and then came home. She mostly kept to herself. One day, though, I came home early, and ... this will sound strange ... she was dressed like a man. Ruby told me she was auditioning for a part at the Footlight Club in Jamaica Plain, where a woman would have to disguise herself as a man."

"You never told me that," said Earl.

"I was afraid you would throw her out!"

"That's what I should have done in the first place!"

Fitzgerald cleared his throat. "We know about the men's clothing," he said. "Lila disguised herself as a Gerard St. Cloud to rent the second apartment and for other nefarious purposes."

"Gerard ... St. Cloud?"

"Do you know the name, Mrs. Preston?"

"Ruby has a half-brother, Gerard, but his last name is Dubois, like hers. He's a handsome rascal."

Earl shot Regina a look.

"I've only met Gerard Dubois twice," Regina said. "Ruby looked up to him, practically worshiped him."

Fitzgerald jotted the name down. "Have you ever seen him in Boston?"

"No, we saw him when we visited our family in Tupelo. May I ask, why the interest in Gerard?"

"We are trying to establish who Lila's partners are. Kidnapping is a serious charge, and we need to know who was involved in the crime." Fitzgerald removed a handkerchief from his jacket pocket and wiped his brow with it. He was starting to feel uncomfortable. Was it the coffee or Mrs. Preston? She seemed like a perfectly nice woman, but could she be controlling his thoughts? How would he know? He shuddered, but remembered that Nicole had vouched for her. Rossi had been his secret weapon, and she had never let him down. Besides, Regina wouldn't be living in a modest apartment like this, if she was bent on controlling the world. He focused again on his interrogation. "Mrs. Preston, did Lila know about your ability?"

"I never told her, Lieutenant. My powers didn't develop until my early 20s. By then I had met Earl, and he urged me not to tell anyone, especially Ruby. He never trusted her." Regina shot a glance at Earl, as though daring him to say "I told you so" again. Her husband remained silent. Mrs. Preston resumed her story. "There was a woman on my father's side, my Aunt May, who had the gift, including the ability to mesmerize. I probably mentioned it in front of Ruby once or twice when we were children, but she never paid much attention to me. She always wanted to be the leader, even in play."

Fitzgerald thought about what had happened after Nicole had done the favor for Kozak, and how a simple mind reading had led to a kidnapping, arrests, and turmoil for everyone concerned. That was probably the type of thing Regina was talking about when she mentioned the consequences of mind control to Nicole. You couldn't know what would happen when you experimented with these things.

Jack returned to the interview. "Mrs. Preston, I don't believe we will need your testimony. You came in touch with your cousin only after the kidnapping. We have other witnesses to make our case."

"What a relief! I'm glad you can rely on other witnesses," Regina said, glancing at Earl and smiling.

It was a relief for Fitzgerald too. Lila's bad break had been a good break for everyone else. When she caught her witch's mask on that window shade, she had revealed her face to Patricia Messina, and Pat could positively identify her now. The ransom note would provide the motive. Even if Laroche started spouting off about a mind reader, no one would take her seriously.

"I'm trying my best to keep the topic of mind reading

out of this case to protect Nicole Rossi," Jack said. "I'm treating her as a confidential informant. I'm assuming that designation will suit you as well."

"That will suit me just fine. Thank you, Lieutenant. I'm glad you understand, and I can tell that you are a good friend to the girl."

I hope I am a good friend, Fitzgerald thought. *I used her to help solve this case. Would I use her again?* Nicole had started the ball rolling with her mind reading, so she had needed to fix that. Now she was out of it. Would he give in to the temptation to take advantage of her skills, if another tough case came along? *No,* he thought, *absolutely not!* But he could already see a flicker of doubt in his mind's eye.

Chapter 28

North End Girl

"This above all: to thine own self be true ..."

— William Shakespeare

Nicole rested her head on a pillow, looking up at the ceiling. For the first time in three weeks, she felt truly at ease. The conversation had gone better than she had expected. When she told her parents she was interested in a young Ukrainian man at work, Mama had paused for a moment and then said an *Abruzzese* equivalent of "well, you're not getting any younger." It was nice to know that her impending status as an old maid, at the ripe old age of 22, had softened up her mother a little. Her father had said, "As long as he's Catholic." Philip was indeed a Catholic, so Nicole could bring her boyfriend out from the shadows at last. *Boyfriend!* She liked the sound of that. Philip wasn't just her friend anymore, he was her boyfriend. She could shout it out loud, but she whispered it instead, since her sister was sleeping.

Everyone had agreed that Nicole should invite Philip over to dinner on Thursday after work. Mama would make Nicole's favorite, spaghetti with meatballs and sausages, and

201

Papa would pick up a rum cake at the bakery for dessert. Would Nicole be too nervous to eat? She hoped not.

She sat up to turn off the light, and glanced at Maria. The pleasant parental reaction was good news for her little sister too, as Maria's future dating life would have fewer limits as well. Her parents wouldn't be able to reverse themselves now, even if Maria didn't turn out to be the "old maid" that Nicole was.

Nicole leaned back and found her pillow again. She thought about how she would tell Philip tomorrow. Some positive news for a change! Maybe she could meet his parents next. Would they invite her over for dinner? *What do Ukrainians eat?* She and Philip had never discussed it. Nicole felt complete happiness as she drifted off to sleep.

"Nicole, Nicole! Wake up! You're having a nightmare," Maria said.

"What?" Nicole realized Maria had been shaking her.

"You kept saying, 'Gerard! Gerard!' That was the name Lila was using, right?"

Nicole rubbed her eyes too roughly, still confused. "Uh, right. Wait, I remember. I was having a dream about someone named Gerard, but he didn't look like Lila, that is, when she was dressed like a man."

"Was it horrible?"

"Not really, but I was still afraid for some reason. I

could see him with Lila, but she looked much younger. I wonder who he is."

"It was just a dream, sis. You know how jumbled dreams can be. I'm sure Lila is still on your mind."

"You're right. I'm okay, Maria. You can go back to sleep."

Maria gave her sister a kiss on the cheek and returned to her bed.

Nicole had spent the evening Lila-free, with thoughts of plans with Philip dancing through her head. Now Lila was pushing those happy reveries aside. Granted, her nemesis was in prison and out of the way, but would Lila mention Nicole's powers to someone there? Might she tell another police officer? Jack wouldn't be the only one to question the prisoner. Probably no one would believe her. Why would anyone believe Lila Laroche, the kidnapper of Mrs. Messina?

Maybe Nicole could talk about it with her new friend Regina Preston. It would be nice to have a confidant who actually possessed similar abilities and might understand her issues better. Yes, Regina had been the blessing in disguise from this ordeal. And Jack. He was the best, but he wouldn't have the perspective that Regina had. Of course, Regina was Lila's cousin. Would Regina harbor any resentment toward Nicole? She hadn't shown any. Everything surrounding Lila was so complicated. It would probably be best to stay away from the subject of Lila, unless Regina brought it up herself. Regina would certainly have other wisdom she could share.

Nicole realized this wasn't the time for such thoughts. She wanted to be fresh when she talked to Philip tomorrow. She began to count backwards from 100 to clear her mind. When she reached the number one, she started over again. Somewhere in the middle of the third round, she drifted off to sleep.

When Nicole arrived at work the next morning, all she could think of was telling Philip the good news about her parents. *He will be so happy*, she thought. When she approached the alcove where the timecards were kept, she spotted a note on her own card. *Not again! What does he want now? It can't be about the Messinas—they've already checked out.* She took a deep breath, remembering the first note which had led to the bad news about Pat's disappearance. Flipping open the folded sheet, she read, "Please see me at once. Lawrence Altman." That didn't tell her much. There was no choice—she'd have to go see him. Nicole went through her usual ritual of brushing down her suit, and set off for the assistant manager's office.

Altman's door was open, and he spotted her before she had a chance to knock. "Come in, Nicole. Please have a seat. I'll be with you in one minute."

Mr. Altman was pleasant and professional, a good supervisor, really, but his pencil-thin mustache always bothered her. She found it oddly unsettling. When he looked up, she quickly averted her eyes.

"Nicole, I believe I have some good news for you."

Good news? Nicole shifted in her seat.

"I have received glowing reports about you from Lieutenant Fitzgerald and the Messinas. They have all talked about your cooperation, professionalism, courtesy, and willingness to help out in whatever way possible. These are just the traits we look for in our staff who are the public face of the Hotel Manger. In evaluating your record over the past two years, with flawless attendance, I might add, and with these outside recommendations in hand, we have decided to promote you to the position of front desk clerk. Of course, you will need training for this position, which will commence a week from today. You will receive an increase of $7.50 per week. I assume you are interested?"

Nicole was thunderstruck. Based on her talks with Jack and the Messinas, she knew that they were sending recommendations for her, but she hadn't really expected a promotion, and to the front desk, no less. She was very excited, but tried to compose herself. There was no sense in ruining this chance by making a bad impression now. She inhaled and let out her breath slowly. "Yes, Mr. Altman, I'm definitely interested. Thank you for this opportunity."

"Wonderful, Nicole. I will set up a training schedule for you later in the week. Check in with me on Friday morning, and I will give it to you then."

"Thank you so much, Mr. Altman."

Altman arose from his chair to shake her hand.

"Congratulations, Nicole."

"Thanks again," she said.

This is unbelievable, she thought, leaving Altman's office. *I'm finally going to get out of that box, and with a good raise to boot! Mama and Papa will be thrilled!* Then she paused. *What will Philip think?* She remembered again that the mind reading favor was supposed to advance Philip's career, not hers. Would this bother him? She would tell him the other good news, about how her parents had reacted to her relationship revelation, first, and then play the rest by ear. She practically skipped to her elevator, as she began another workday at the Hotel Manger.

Nicole met Philip for their morning break. *Won't it be wonderful when I can spend more time with Philip outside of work,* she thought. She couldn't hide her happiness and excitement.

"Look at you! You're beaming! Must be good news," said Philip.

"The best! You are invited to dinner on Thursday after work! I hope you're not working a double shift!"

"I'm not! This is wonderful! What happened?"

Nicole explained how her parents had softened on their "Italians only" policy for prospective suitors. "I always complain about their old-fashioned ways, but I think it worked to our advantage this time. They figure I'm getting old, so they can't be too choosy."

"You're not old. That's ridiculous."

"Thank you, but let's just accept this as a gift. Now, to the dinner. We're going to have spaghetti, meatballs, and sausages for supper, and Papa will buy a rum cake. Wear something nice."

"Should I wear a suit?"

"It wouldn't hurt. Mama appreciates a nice appearance. She's going to love you, I just know it!" Philip looked as happy as she was, so Nicole didn't have the heart to tell him about her promotion. The news would keep, for now, but she would have to tell him soon, and definitely before Monday. She knew he wouldn't mope for too long, but Nicole didn't want to spoil this moment. They just kept smiling at each other.

Tuesday came and went, and Nicole still hadn't told Philip about her promotion. She was consumed with thoughts of the Thursday dinner and how it would go with her parents. She didn't want any problems with Philip to intrude on the evening, which might be important for their future together. Maybe he would take her promotion news well, but what if he didn't? Nicole decided she would tell him on Friday, after what she hoped would be a pleasant dinner. She wouldn't begin training on the new job until Monday, so he would still know in time.

Nicole met Philip for lunch in the hotel's coffee shop on Wednesday. They usually brought their lunches from home to save money, but decided to splurge as a little celebration of the good news from her parents.

Just Nicole's luck, their waitress was June again. June was a bit too flirty with Philip. *Shouldn't she be more professional?* Nicole wondered.

June gave her head a not-so-subtle shake, advertising her blond curls. "Hey, Philip ... Nicole. I usually don't see you two at lunchtime."

"We are treating ourselves today," said Philip.

"Is this because of Nicole's promotion?"

Oh, no! Nicole thought. *How did she find out? I guess waitresses overhear a lot of gossip.* Another reason not to like June.

Philip looked at Nicole. "Yeah, that's the reason, her promotion."

Nicole mouthed the word "sorry" to Philip.

"Okay, kids, what'll you have for the celebration lunch?"

"I'll have a cheeseburger and a Coca-Cola," said Philip.

"I'll have a tuna fish sandwich and a Coke," said Nicole.

"Anything for dessert?"

"No," said Philip. "We have only 30 minutes."

"I'll get this right in," said June. She gave Philip a little pinch on his arm, and turned on her heel.

Philip didn't waste any time after June left. "What's this about a promotion?"

"I'm sorry I didn't tell you, honey. I was so happy about the news from my parents. I was going to tell you on Friday, after we got the dinner with them behind us."

"I said I was a little jealous, but I would get over it. You could have told me."

"I'm sorry, I should have. Please don't be cross with me. I was just trying to keep things simple until after the dinner. I should have had more faith in you."

"You should have." Philip looked at her, and surprised her with a smile. "It's okay. I understand. This was a lot to deal with in one week. We will be all right, don't worry. So, what's the new job?"

Nicole saw June coming with their Cokes, so she waited until the waitress had left. Nicole described the new position to Philip, and he said he was proud of her. He seemed sincere. Nicole had told Fitzgerald that Philip was a good guy, and she was right. This experience gave her even more confidence that her parents would also see that Philip was the right man for her. Her mistake had turned into another blessing in disguise.

But, really, she could do without that June.

Nicole waited for Philip in the Manger's lobby after work on Thursday. He was changing out of his bellhop's uniform, and she was hoping whatever he had chosen to wear would make a good impression on her parents. When he walked around the corner from the staff area, she almost gasped. He looked like a million bucks— gray suit, white shirt, and a red and black striped tie. On top of that, he was carrying a bouquet of yellow and white carnations.

"Are those for me?" Nicole asked.

"They're for your mother."

"Even better. She will love them." Nicole took Philip's arm. "You look so handsome. She will love you too."

"What about your father?"

"Let's just shoot for 'like' with him right now."

"Good enough."

Exiting through the front door of the hotel onto Causeway Street, Philip asked, "How will this language thing work?"

"They have some basic English, but I will have to translate anything more complicated. I've told Maria to help out too."

"Good. I need all the help I can get."

"It will be fine, honey. I've probably made them out to be worse than they are."

"You have made them sound a little scary." Philip grabbed her hand tighter.

They are a little scary, Nicole thought, but she didn't share that observation with Philip.

They walked from the Manger to the North End of Boston, Nicole's home for her entire life. She knew the tenement housing like the back of her hand, but she began to look at the area with new eyes. It didn't seem like a place that was holding her back anymore. This was her neighborhood, which she could truly share with Philip now, introducing him to her culture without concern that nosy neighbors might catch sight of them. She could take him to the Feast of St. Anthony in August, with its myriad sights and sounds—bright confetti, spirited music, happy voices—a vibrant pageant of life. They could hold hands as they walked among the stalls, and she would introduce Philip to any neighbors she met.

The couple turned off of Endicott Street to Thacher, passing the brick façade and sweet aromas of Regina Pizza. How she would love to sit in one of their wooden booths with her guy. She could do that now too.

Onward to Prince Street, and finally to Baldwin Place. Mama had swept the stairs. She always swept the stairs when guests we're coming. Someday maybe Philip wouldn't be a guest.

Up the steps, into the hallway, and through the apartment door.

"Mama, papa, we're here!"

Inspirations, Acknowledgments, and Historical Notes

Almost all the characters in *North End Girl* are figments of my imagination, but the character of Nicole Rossi was inspired by my mother, Hilda Siraco Romanko. Mom was an elevator operator at the Hotel Manger around the same time that fictional Nicole would have been there. A couple of Nicole's stories, such as the one where her photo appeared in the *Boston Traveler*, petting a rooster, no less, came from my mother. I still have the tattered clipping that Mom cherished all those years ago. To the best of my knowledge, however, my mother wasn't a mind reader, although you had to wonder sometimes. Most of the other aspects of Nicole's life I manufactured as well. Mom, for example, lived in East Cambridge rather than the North End, which also had an Italian community, and was chosen as the setting for Nicole's home because of its proximity to the Hotel Manger.

As to the places described in the novel, I have tried to stick to the historical record as closely as possible. The real Hotel Manger, like the fictional one, was located on Causeway Street in Boston, adjacent to both North Station and Boston Garden. I found several brochures for the hotel on eBay, one describing it as "The Wonder Hotel of New England." The brochures provided photos of the lobby, lounge, dining room, etc., which helped to flesh out my descriptions. Librarians in the Research Services department at the Boston Public Library came to my rescue with fire insurance maps, which answered other questions I had, such as where the elevators were located in the lobby. My cousin Daniel White provided news articles and videos about the history of the Manger, published around the time that the hotel, then called the Hotel Madison, was demolished in 1983. That beautiful hotel, with all its stories to tell and memories to evoke, is no more.

The character of Lila Laroche was completely my creation, but the row houses where she lived have real-life counterparts on Phillips Street, as does the secret tunnel she used to make her escape. In the "truth is stranger than fiction" department, there is in fact a remnant of a secret tunnel on Phillips Street, which was used by the members of the Underground Railroad during the 1860s. I've been attracted to the idea of secret passages and tunnels since I was a kid, so I wanted to include one in my book. I started searching Google for real tunnels in Boston, which I had assumed would be the remains of bootlegger tunnels from Prohibition during the 1920s. When I came across an article about an actual tunnel used by members of the Underground Railroad, I couldn't believe my eyes. According to a 2023 piece at nbcboston.com, The Hayden House, located on Phillips Street and once a safe house along the Underground Railroad route, still has a portion of a formerly secret tunnel used by escaped slaves to enter and leave the residence without being seen. The Fugitive Slave Acts, federal laws that allowed for the capture and return of runaway enslaved people, also applied to free states such as Massachusetts, where bounty hunters would search for escaped slaves. Secret tunnels, such as the one on Phillips Street, helped the escapees to stay one step ahead of bounty hunters.

In addition to the tunnel story, Lila's grandmother told her about female slaves who had disguised themselves as men to escape captivity, and Lila took that story to heart in inventing her Gerard St. Cloud persona. Nan's disguised slave story also has historical analogues, as when Ellen Craft disguised herself as a disabled white gentleman to escape from slavery in 1848. She and her soon-to-be husband William Craft, who pretended to be her servant, found freedom in Boston and lived for two years at The Hayden House, as described in the nbcboston.com article. History has some amazing, important, and moving stories to tell.

Companies and businesses in Boston that became part of the novel, such as Jordan Marsh, the Paramount Theatre, Bailey's Ice Cream, and Regina Pizza, existed in the real Boston of the time on the streets mentioned in the book. The walking and public transportation routes the characters took were verified in primary sources of the period. My husband, Bob Desharnais, gave me the following wonderful and useful resources as Christmas gifts, which assisted in my research: the 1949 *Classified Telephone Directory* for Boston and Vicinity, the

Everywhere in Boston and How to Get There Street Guide, and a vintage street map. Although I grew up in Boston myself, I wasn't there in 1949, and these sources helped confirm that the places I remembered did exist during the period in which the novel takes place. Bob also listened as I read each chapter of my first draft aloud, providing encouragement and feedback throughout the writing process. He has always been my wellspring of strength, support, and love.

My dad, William Romanko, was an inspiration for the character of Philip, although young Mr. Kozak is highly fictionalized. While my dad did indeed have blue-gray eyes, he was never a bellhop at the Manger. Dad did, however, work at Gentles Baking Company in Mattapan, so I chose that as the focal point for the "Lila in exile" chapters. I grew up in Mattapan, but I again wanted to make sure that the businesses I remembered and described in the story were actually there before I arrived. The primary sources mentioned above helped me with that, and the librarians at the BPL again came to my aid with an atlas map that showed the external layout of Gentles in that era. *Mattapan Through Time* (America Through Time, 2023), a photo book by Anthony M. Sammarco, provided backup for other Mattapan locations, such as the branch library on Hazelton Street.

While writing the book, I was mindful of the language that would have been used in 1949. Women were often called "girls" at the time in both formal and informal settings. My research revealed, for example, a 1940s advertisement in the

Boston Globe for "Elevator Girls" at the Hotel Manger. Calling women "girls" in the workplace extended well into my own lifetime.

Black people were called "colored" or "Negro" during that period. A 2014 article at NPR.org notes that "The use of the phrase 'colored people' peaked in books published in 1970." While most, including yours truly, prefer to use different words today, I wanted to stay true to what people would have said in 1949 Boston.

While some things can and should change, others should endure. Several of the places I mentioned in the novel still exist in the Boston of today, and at the same locations. Among them are Boston Common, the exquisite Public Garden, Regina Pizza (now Pizzeria), Emmanuel College, Fenway Park, and Jamaica Pond.

May we always find in our lives the perfect balance of past histories, present realities, and future hopes.

Karen A. Romanko

Los Angeles, California
May 2025